# CALI BOYS

Also by Kelli London

*The Break-Up Diaries, Vol. 1* (with Ni-Ni Simone)

*Boyfriend Season*

*Uptown Dreams*

Published by Kensington Publishing Corporation

# CALI BOYS

## *A Boyfriend Season Novel*

# KELLI LONDON

Dafina KTeen Books
KENSINGTON PUBLISHING CORP.
http://www.kensingtonbooks.com

Cali Boys *is dedicated to two very important people in my life. Two incredible ladies who are so much more than my friends: you both make up my dynamic duo, and are the best from-the-soul sisters a girl could ask for.*

*Lashon Fryer, my "sister" since kindergarten: Without you I wouldn't have completed this book. Thanks for being just a phone call away, and answering even when you're extremely busy and do not have the heart to say so, because that's what we do as family—we're there no matter what or when. When you need me, I'm on standby. ☺*

*Linda Washington-Johnson, my spiritual soul sister: Priceless, ever ready, and never wavering in your truth, friendship, and loyalty are just a few ways to describe you. Thank you for your honesty and always being yourself.*

*Cheers to you both!*

# Acknowledgments

A huge thanks to my princess and princes: T, CII, and K. You three are, hands down, the best of the best. You're extremely intelligent, good-hearted, and selfless. You give me three reasons to smile every morning, laugh every day, and love you even more each night. Love you. Love you. Love you. ;)

For my family and friends: Thank you for supporting and encouraging me. You all are wonderful. Don't ever forget it. I thank you.

Huge kudos and many hugs to my dream team of consultants in New York, Atlanta, and Philadelphia: Rukiya "Kiki" Murray, Alakea Woods, Josh "UnconQUErable" Woods, Chris Ferreras, and Eligio "E" a/k/a "Zap" Bailey. You are all priceless!

Thanks to my fellow writers who offer wonderful teen readers an escape and entertainment. I am proud to be a part of the movement.

Selena James: Your vision and dedication are incredible! Thank you for believing in my characters and stories as much as I do. With your help, I've brought many to life. Now let's get ready for *Epic Fiascos*!

For my readers, I truly and humbly thank you with all of my heart. You're incredible, appreciated, and top of tops. Let's rock the world together!

## From Kelli

'Tis the season for boys, boys, and more boys. That's what the world thinks most teenage girls think of, right? Wrong! Okay, well, sometimes, I guess, at least in *Cali Boys*. However, there's so much more to a girl's mind and heart. While writing this book, I was forced to address a lot of problems that teen girls encounter, in addition to their boyfriend issues (or the lack thereof, because sometimes a girl just hasn't snagged the right guy yet): friend issues and disloyalty, a girl's rite of passage into womanhood, weight problems, bullying, and, of course, one of my favorites—self-esteem. We, as girls (some of us are a bit more mature, like me, but still girls at heart ☺), have a lot of day-to-day realities and problems to overcome. And while many will be trying, or seem a tad hard to bear, believe me, there's a beautiful trade-off on the other side. There's always a lesson to be learned, and that lesson, a jewel of life, is the reward. In short, our lives aren't just what we make them; our lives are about what lessons we learn, then apply, to better ourselves. Because that is always the point, my jewel of a friend: bettering yourself.

So while I've penned this book to entertain you, please read the lessons between the lines. Despite what others may think of you, it's what you think of yourself that really counts. So think you are the best. Meditate on excellence, education, having a good heart and being a great person. And remember: it's not what you are called, it's what you answer to. You are royalty, and you should always be addressed as Your Highness (<u>your</u> <u>name</u> <u>here</u>)—even if it's only in your mind—because whatever a girl thinketh, she can become!

TTYL my fellow Queens!

Take care. Be strong. Love yourself.

Your girl,

Kells, aka Royal Highness, Kelli London

(See how I filled in the blank with my name?

I'm with you!)

KelliLondon.com

# WELCOME TO THE NEIGHBORHOOD

# 1

# JACOBI SWANSON

*It's not supposed to happen this way*, Jacobi stressed, sloshing a creamy mask on her face, then washing her hands and drying them on her jeans before getting down to business. *It's just not.* With her damp fingers, she pinched the shirt fabric where her breasts were supposed to be, then pulled, making two lopsided, sideways tepees. She'd never have melon-sized brassiere-fillers like her best friend, Katydid, and definitely wouldn't have vavoom-sized, D cup ta-tas like the women in her family. Her head shook at the thought. Never mind large. Big ones didn't matter so much. The problem was, it seemed as if she'd never have enough to fill a bra. At least not in the equal sense. Her small breasts were different sizes. One was clearly bigger than the other, by almost an inch. The other was barely a lump.

"This is ridiculous," she said, letting the shirt snap

back against her skin, leaving wet fingerprints where she'd pulled. The unevenness made her more insecure. How was she supposed to start a new school in a couple of months looking like her left boob had been deflated? She nodded. It would take some serious work and dedication to even out her breasts before summer was over, but she'd do it—whatever it was. And *it*—the solution—lay before her on the sink in a magazine whose cover touted BOOB LIFT OR BUST: 2 BEST CHEST EXERCISES. Turning to page sixty-three, Jacobi read the directions, took off her shirt, and grabbed a medium-sized hand towel. "I can do this. I will do this. I *must* do this."

Her left hand gripped one end of the towel; her right, the other. She pulled, tugging on the terry cloth until she felt her chest muscles tighten, then released. Again she performed the routine, pulling for a second, then letting go. She repeated the exercise in short intervals, tightening and loosening in quick, five-second repetitions while she watched her muscles contract in the mirror. They'd barely moved, she noted. But they had, and that caused her to smile.

"Pull to the east. Pull to the west . . . to increase your breasts! To the east. To the west. To increase your breasts!" She sang a bit too loudly, switching her hips side to side in rhythm with her words, mimicking a dance she and Katydid made up years ago.

Jacobi turned sideways and viewed herself in the mirror. Her profile hadn't changed one bit, but she felt like it had. With a solid thirty days of the bust-increasing exercise, she was sure she'd see a difference. And she hoped it'd be sooner than later because the four marks where she'd pulled on her shirt, two on either side of where bigger breasts were supposed to be, stood out more than anything else on her chest. That was a definite no-no. Girls her age—in her opinion—were supposed to have something to look at. Namely, boobs.

"To the east. To the west . . ." she sang again, then paused mid mantra, sure she saw and heard the doorknob rattle. "I'm in here!" she yelled.

A deep laugh rumbled from outside the bathroom. "To the north. To the south. Now get your butt out!" Diggs, her older brother, answered. "That's why nobody likes you but Katydid, Jacobi. You're weird. Mean and weird. 'To the east. To the west . . .' Who says stuff like that? And you wonder why you can't make new friends?"

"Yeah!" said her younger brother, Hunter, agreeing with anything that Diggs said, as usual. He was barely five, and already a huge toothpick in her side.

"Shut up!" Jacobi's heart raced, and a film of perspiration made the creamy cleanser mask run down the sides of her face to her neck. Just the mention of her not making new friends made her panic even more. If she had a choice—which she didn't—she'd have plenty of friends in the new neighborhood; that's what she told herself. But the truth was, here she was a loner—an unsocial butterfly who longed for her old stomping grounds and her real BFFs, Katydid and Shooby, though Shooby was more of a crush than a best friend. But not having friends here wasn't her fault. Where she came from, you had to either stand on your own or join some dumb female clique that paraded as a gang. And getting into trouble wasn't her thing, but she knew she could hold her own and hang with the best of the troublemakers if forced to; she and Katydid had done so plenty of times together. The housing projects had taught her that. And it didn't matter that they'd moved to a house where they didn't have to have bars on their windows. The lessons of the streets were already ingrained in her mind, and it was too late to erase them. So, she wondered, how was she responsible for any aspect of her new life? She was in friendless surroundings, had been forced to move into a new neighborhood where she didn't know anyone, and was broke compared to all the other teens in her area. More importantly, she questioned, how much had her older brother heard? She wiped away the white, creamy facial mask streaks from her skin and tried to wish Diggs away.

A loud banging on the door told her that wishing-away powers were only real in movies, and served as an answer to her wondering how much Diggs had heard.

"Increase your breasts on your own time, in your own room," Diggs said, laughing between words. "The truly grown folk—like me—need to use the bathroom. I gotta get fresh, too, before the motorcycle show tomorrow. That's why you're trying to magically grow breastesses overnight, right?"

Before she knew it, she'd swiped her things off the counter and opened the door. She was embarrassed and upset, mad that she had to share a bathroom with her brother. If her parents weren't such penny-pinchers, they'd have sprung for a house with more rooms instead of moving to Baldwin Hills and banking half the small in-heritance they'd received upon her grandmother's death. Who wanted to live in the Hills, anyway? She'd have set-tled for someplace on the outskirts of Los Angeles where people weren't so uppity. She shrugged. Maybe if they'd had the money they had now—money she'd been secretly flipping for her father on Wall Street for the last few weeks, ever since he'd caught her trading penny stocks—she could've changed their minds by changing their bot-tom line: their debt-to-income ratio and net worth.

"What, you think growing bigger breasts is gonna keep your singer boyfriend, Shooby?" he asked, laugh-ing. "Shoo-shoo-shoo shooby-do," he sang. "I hear he can't even sing."

"Shut up, Diggs! And for your information, he's not a singer. Shooby's just his nickname. You don't know what you're talking about," she snapped, pushing him out of her way and into the almost ceiling-high pile of moving boxes they hadn't yet unpacked. Yes, he was right; she'd hoped she could puff out her chest a bit. She wanted to look like the other girls in their crew, and was sure Shooby would finally notice her if she did. She didn't want to be invisible and stay in the background; she wanted some-one to pay attention to her at the motorcycle show. And not just any someone, but Shooby, the only person from her old Lancaster neighborhood besides Katydid that she was sure she'd never be able to let go of. They had a his-tory together; one that included flash mobbing for fun, Scooby tutoring her on life, and Jacobi liking him.

Suddenly Diggs snatched the magazine from under her

arm. He held it up as high as he could while he scanned the cover.

"Give it back!" Jacobi yelled, jumping in an effort to take it from him. But that's all it was—effort. Diggs was tall, skyscraper-high for his age, and she couldn't reach the magazine no matter how high she bounced. "Stop playing, Diggs!" She drew back and punched him squarely in the chest.

"Ow," he said, pretending she had hurt him. "Breast exercises. Hmm." He cackled like a hyena. "Girl, you better pray. Ask God to fix your teeth and face first—your breasts can come later. First you need to be pro-active. Get it? Like the acne stuff," he said, laughing and pushing his way into the bathroom, tossing the magazine at Jacobi right before he slammed the door in her face. "Or just keep hiding behind the stock market and that stupid video camera you love so much. Those are your friends. As long as you're behind the lens of that camera or the *Wall Street Journal*, and not on video or the front page, you won't be harming the world," he yelled.

She poked out her lips, begged herself not to cry, and wished she and God could have a two-way conversation so she could know for certain what He was planning for her. Diggs was right. Her skin was atrocious, her breasts were lopsided, and the prized video camera her father had surprised her with was her only close friend now, es-pecially since the stock market was plummeting and she was constantly losing money. But prayer wasn't the only thing she needed—that she knew for sure, because she'd kneeled down many times to ask God for at least a B cup. She needed help from a different sort of trinity: divine intervention from a higher power, heavenly chest exercises, and an angel for a dermatologist. And because their flash-mob crew was growing thicker by the day, and Shooby was the ringleader with all eyes on him—girls' eyes—she knew she needed immediate help to get his attention.

# 2

# KASSIDY MADDOX

The Beverly Center was crowded, as usual, and Kassidy was peeved. She pushed through the throng of mall shoppers, hating Los Angeles more and more with each shove she gave and each pleasantry some polite stranger returned. *Why is everyone so nice here?* "La-La Land," she muttered, answering her own question as she made her way to the escalator, ignoring a phone call from an unknown caller. "Why do I have to live here?" she asked for the umpteenth time, seeing no reason for the twenty-five-hundred-mile move from New York to Cali. Sure, her mother had eloped with an LA local, but, as far as Kassidy was concerned, her mother's marriage and relocation had nothing to do with her. One, she didn't really know her new daddy dearest and hadn't preapproved him, though she'd put on a pretense to make her mom happy because her mother was deserving of happiness. Two, New York was her playground, and, for her, there was no place like the Big Apple. Three, Manhattan was where she'd made all of her money by being a highly sought-after teen model. Growing up, the rule had been that Mommy was the manager and Kassidy was the star, but not after today. In the last twenty-four hours, she'd waved good-bye to her friends and boyfriend, Brent, hopped a plane from John F. Kennedy International Airport to LAX, and now she was here at the mall on a guilt-trip shopping spree, courtesy of her mom. She shrugged. She didn't know what made her mother think that more clothes and shoes could erase the headache and heartache moving had caused Kassidy, but, whatever it was, her mom was wrong. Flat-out wrong. But she'd accept the new wardrobe as a gift, though it wouldn't be enough to sway her. Kassidy had been on modeling shoots in Los Angeles too many times to count, and she'd frequented the Beverly Center, Rodeo Drive, Santa Monica, and other trendy places more than she'd care to admit, and not one had made her want to stay. New York pulsed through her veins, plain and simple, and she was certain she'd die without the heartbeat of the city of all cities. More than longing for New York and everything that came with it, she missed the love of her life, Brent— the boyfriend of all boyfriends. He was the one she'd kept, the only one she was true to, except for when he wasn't looking. But what boys didn't know didn't hurt them. That's what she'd told herself. Now she wished she'd been faithful and spent more time with him. Maybe being forced to move was the universe's way of paying her back for cheating. Karma.

Her phone vibrated again, and "Unknown Caller"

popped up on the screen. As always, she pressed Ignore, wondering why whoever-it-was kept calling anonymously. She always treated anonymous calls the same: she didn't take them.

As Kassidy approached the escalator, she saw that a small crowd had gathered, and she stopped behind it. Someone appeared to be blocking the escalator. As though her hand were a magic wand, she extended it between two boys and parted the group of people who seemed to be way more tolerant than she.

"Excuse me," Kassidy said to the back of some extra-large girl who wasn't moving. Kassidy was simultaneously reading a text from Faith, her best friend in Los Angeles, who said that she was waiting for her on the top floor. Faith was also a model, one that Kassidy had helped many times; in fact, she had just hooked her up with a major shoot in New York. Faith wasn't on the same level as Kassidy, but she knew the ropes in California and had promised to introduce Kassidy to all the bigwigs she needed to know. *It'll be nice to have someone to talk shop with here*, Kassidy thought, then realized the person blocking the elevator hadn't moved a centimeter. "Excuse me," Kassidy repeated, not sure if the girl had heard her. Her phone vibrated in her hand again, stealing her attention. A message from Brent came through: **CALL ME.**

She called him immediately. When a song met her ears, she was certain she had the wrong number. She hung up. Brent didn't do any sort of ringtones or music on his phone. She shrugged, then scrolled to his name in

Favorites and selected it. Again, some song came on. Kassidy gave it a few seconds and was about to hang up.

"Hey. You like it?" Brent asked.

"What?" Kassidy said, smiling for no reason.

"The song that you heard when you called. That's mine. I'm thinking of becoming a double threat, a model and singer-songwriter. I've been dabbling with my boy at the studio, and we're putting some tracks together. Maybe we can get one of the designers to use it during Fashion Week," he said.

Kassidy smiled, walking forward, then bumped into the rude girl, the one who was blocking the escalator. "Uh . . . I said excuse me. Didn't you hear?"

The girl glanced over her shoulder, sucked her teeth in irritation, and turned back around. She'd rotated her head so quickly, Kassidy didn't get a good look at her, but her message was clear: she didn't care.

"S'cuse me. S'cuse me," the girl mimicked, messing up the enunciation. She stepped sideways, positioning herself in the middle of the escalator. She obviously had no intention of moving, and purposely stood in the way of everyone who tried to politely get by her. "Excuse yourself, skinny girl . . . right outta my way. Maybe if you had asked me nicer, I'd move. So *you* move. I was here first."

Kassidy couldn't believe the nerve of the girl. "Baby, I'm going to call you after I finish shopping," she said.

"Wait, Kassidy. Make sure you call because I won't be able to text—" he began.

"Later," Kassidy said, cutting him off and pressing END on the phone. She wasn't able to really hear what he'd said because the rude girl kept talking trash. She put her hand on her hip and asked the girl once more to move. The girl turned completely around, and Kassidy almost threw up in her own mouth. The girl had a white ring of confectionary sugar around her chapped lips and a dab of what appeared to be jelly on her chin, courtesy of the huge powdered doughnut she scarfed. Without a hint of embarrassment, the girl licked the reddish filling off her fingers, looking Kassidy up and down. Kassidy took a good look at the girl's face, and almost keeled over. The girl had two faint black marks on her cheeks where blush would've normally been, and she didn't breathe; she snored while awake. Kassidy almost cringed at the sound of the heavy wheeze.

"You should see about that," Kassidy said, and tried to move the girl out of the way with the back of her hand. It was bad enough that she was here in La-La Land, but her good friend and only connection to the modeling world was waiting. From Kassidy's experience, cash and opportunity didn't wait on anyone, and if something didn't make money, it didn't make cents or sense.

"S'cuse me?" The girl pushed Kassidy's hand away, then stepped in front of her. "I know you didn't! And see about what, Ms. Lookin' Like Feed The Children?" she spat between bites of the doughnut.

Kassidy paused, looking down at her hand. She couldn't believe the girl had the nerve to lay a jelly-smudged finger on her. *Where is my sanitizer? Where is my sanitizer?* "I said"—she paused for effect and looked the girl dead-on— "you should see about your snorting—I mean, wheezing. And the rings on your cheeks? Oh yeah, you should get 'em checked out, too—they're signs of insulin problems, probably from obesity. Maybe if you put down the doughnut and learned about nutrition, you'd know. And, roly-poly, if anyone looks like Feed The Children, it's your fault. Obviously, you've depleted the world's food supply in one sitting." She pressed her foot onto the ground to steady herself, successfully pushed the mean girl out of the way, and hopped on the escalator with head held high. The girl hadn't put an ounce of fear in her at all. Kassidy was a New Yorker. Sugar-lipped, round, jelly-faced foodies didn't scare her.

"Wait until I catch you," the girl threatened from the bottom of the escalator. "LA's small. We'll see each other again."

Kassidy's hand was on her hip, and her neck snaked. "Ms. Snack Attack, for my eyes' sake, I hope not. But whatever." She shrugged. "I'm not running. You can find me in one of the stores that don't sell your size because, I'm sure, no one sells size elephant." She turned her head, hoping to spot either Faith or her mother. She needed to shop until she dropped.

Armed with only four shopping bags, Kassidy hadn't found enough suitable items to put a dent in her disdain for LA, but she knew better than to show it. She plastered a huge smile on her face and nodded at her mom as they exited the store. "I'm telling you, the girl's attitude was as huge as she was. Had the nerve to be standing in front of the escalator stuffing a jelly doughnut down her trap, not letting anyone by. Not even the elderly," Kassidy told her mom and Faith.

"Oh God," Faith chimed in, shaking her waist-length blond-highlighted tresses. Disgust was on her face when she pushed up her perfect brows. "Sugar? She can't be a true Los Angeles girl. We don't do sugar here—or extra weight. Unless, of course, she's Eastie, like the raggedy hood rats from the east side. You know, base. Only bottom-feeders—the non-elite—scarf doughnuts." She pushed her arm through Kassidy's, hooking them together like they were sisters. "Speaking of bottom-feeders, did I tell you my people hooked me up with another urban shoot in New York? Thanks to you and the hookup you gave me, of course. I leave tomorrow."

Kassidy and her mother frowned.

"What does an urban shoot have to do with bottom-feeders? Urban is anything within city limits, right?" Kassidy asked, almost turned off by Faith's judgment about urban people. She was urban, and so were her family and boyfriend. Then her eyes lit. Faith was going to New York, where Brent was. Maybe she could find a way to go with. Since she hadn't unpacked yet, she could just grab one of her bags. It would be easy travel, she believed.

Faith laughed. "If you saw where we're shooting, you'd understand. I'm talking super ghetto. I bet you'd see a bunch of greasy whales like the girl you're talking about. Just déclassé!"

Kassidy laughed for two reasons. One, because she didn't want to do anything that would make Faith not want to include her on the trip. Two, the rude girl did resemble a whale, that was for sure. "Well, she certainly is a huge mammal who clearly likes confections. She was just big and ugly for no reason."

Kassidy's mom grimaced. "Kass, don't use words like that. It's rude to call heavier people huge." She stopped dead in her tracks, then looked around the mall like she'd lost something.

Kassidy almost walked into her. "Uh, Mom? Why not? If big girls call me skinny, then why can't I call them big? Prejudice works on both sides, big and small. And what are you looking for?"

Her mother turned around. "Well, it's a sort of a surprise. Sort of because I didn't tell you she was meeting us here, but I told you your stepdad had a daughter, but, obviously, you didn't listen. Anyway, I think you two will get along just fine. Rather, I'm hoping you *three*," she began, looking from Kassidy to Faith, holding her stare to make her point. "Hopefully you all will pull it off. Different can be a good thing."

"You know, Faith, I could go with you to New York and help you out a little. Even introduce you to some more people . . ."

Her mother shook her head and tsk-tsked. "Uh, no. I know what you're up to. And it's not just modeling; it's that boyfriend of yours. Maybe next time. Right now—today, tomorrow, or for as long as it takes—I need you to meet and learn about your new family."

Kassidy's jaw dropped. She wasn't ready to get to know the new daddy dearest yet. Not until she'd racked up enough things to pacify her and figured out a way to get back to New York and Brent, since her mother had killed her latest dream. "But we've already met. Remember when he flew in to take you to dinner?"

"Uh-uh," her mom answered, just to be saying something. She was clearly not paying attention. "Oh, wait. Ah, yes. Here she comes."

"*She?*" Kassidy asked, shooting a quizzical look at Faith.

"Yes," her mother said, clapping like a cheerleader, then pointing. "I always wanted you to have a sister—"

"Sister?" Kassidy parroted. What was her mom talking about?

"Yummy! Over here, sweetie," her mom called out, waving.

"*Yummy?*" Kassidy craned her neck to see where her mom was pointing, and her stomach fell to her knees. She was sure she was going to regurgitate in her own mouth this time. *Oh. No.* That *will never be my sister*, she thought as she locked eyes with none other than Ms. Snack Attack herself, complete with the powdered-sugar ring still around her chapped lips.

"Oh God. That's your new sister?" Faith asked in total disbelief and even more disgust. "I bet you really wish you could go with, now."

Kassidy shook her head vehemently. "She'll never be my sister. And since I can't go, I'll need a favor. I need you to find my boyfriend. Quick!" She most definitely had to get back to New York, ASAP.

# 3

## JACOBI

"Dear God, I know you can hear me. But are you listening? Please send a sign that you are. I've done everything I'm supposed to do. I haven't lied. Well, not really, except to Diggs. Okay, and maybe to my parents about liking this new house and neighborhood and not sneaking back to my old neighborhood in Lancaster. But that was only once. Okay, twice. Okay, okay, already. Three times. Please forgive me for those, but I was looking for Katydid, and I couldn't find her, but you already know that. Right, God? And also forgive me for pushing Hunter down, but he deserved it, God, he did. So, God, if you could find it in your big heart to give me a pass, can you please send me some breasts and an acne cure, and make the stock market rise? Oh, and a few great shots would be nice, too. I've been trying to perfect working with the new video camera Dad surprised me with, so if you could send a great idea so I can come up with a short film, that'd be great. Thank you, God."

Jacobi got up from bended knees and dusted them off. She hated the hardwood floors in the new house, along with just about every other thing her parents loved so much. She shrugged. She'd just have to get over it, at least for the next three years or so, until she went to college; that's what Shooby and Katydid had said. She was only fifteen, which meant she had no say about where they lived because she didn't pay the mortgage.

A soft knock on her door told her that her mom was on the other side. Her dad was usually the only one in the house who respected her privacy, probably because Jacobi was a girl, and girls, according to him, needed space for girl time and girl things—*things* meaning stuff she wasn't yet ready for, like monthly feminine supplies; but she'd never tell him that, or her mother, for that matter. But her dad wasn't home, and Diggs and Hunter just barged in whenever they felt like it, so she knew it had to be her mom. Her mother had taken to politeness lately, just as she'd taken to all things that she considered upper-class, now that they'd moved, including being proactive in her daughter's education—something she'd never done before because she'd had to work all the time.

"Hey, sweetie," her mom said with a huge smile plastered across her face. "There's someone at the door for you."

Jacobi's eyebrows shot to the ceiling and her eyes rolled. She didn't know anyone in the neighborhood and preferred to keep it that way. "For me? Who?" she asked, sucking her teeth.

Still smiling, her mother shrugged and raised her brows. Jacobi noticed that somehow her forehead wrinkles had magically disappeared. Her mother held her hand to her chest in an *oh my* fashion. "Alissa—I think that's what she said her name is. 'Alissa with one *l*, an *i*, and two *s*'s'. That's what she said. Guess that means *A-l-i-s-s-a*, I think. Anyway, she's waiting on the porch. Also, before you go, don't forget to check into that film class I found. It's recurrent. It starts every eight weeks."

Jacobi stared at her mother's smooth forehead and pursed her lips together in thought. All it took was two seconds for her to think about it. No, she wasn't going to a stupid film class. Not unless she could take an investment class, too, which her mom said she couldn't because she thought it was a waste of time. She didn't know Jacobi had been making money on the market, and Jacobi couldn't tell her. Legally, Jacobi was too young to trade, and there was no way her mom would allow her to. Jacobi shrugged. *Whatever.* She didn't know an Alissa, and had never heard of one. And definitely didn't know anyone who went around spelling out their name.

"What happened to your face? Your wrinkles disappeared. And are you sure the girl's not looking for Diggs? All the girls—for whatever reason; bad taste, maybe?—look for him."

Her mother's eyebrows rose higher, then she purposely moved them up and down. "Ah, you noticed. I had Botox, sweetie. All the women around here do it. And sorry to disappoint you, sweetie, but no. She's here for you." Her mother smiled wider, apparently glad someone was visiting Jacobi. "Now, don't be rude, Jacobi. She seems really nice. She's a . . . bit . . . well, uh, different, but nice."

Jacobi gave herself the once-over in the mirror, wondering what *different* meant and hoping God had already cured her boob and acne problem. But no-go. He hadn't worked as fast as she would've liked on the physical thing, so maybe that meant He had her covered on the creative request for a good documentary idea. She looked to the ceiling, closed her eyes for a second, and gently reminded Him of her prayer, then grabbed her purse and video camera. She was heading out to the motorcycle show to meet Shooby. Today was supposed to be their day alone, which, at first, she thought was unusual because she couldn't remember their ever being together without the crew being around. But he'd stressed that they—and they alone—needed to hook up because he had something to tell her. She only hoped it was that he felt the same as she did. She fingered her new camera, thinking that filming a few minutes of the bikes and people would be good, too. Maybe she could get Shooby to commentate, like a television journalist, before they snuck away together, so she figured meeting this Alissa girl couldn't be a total waste of time since she had to leave through the front door anyway.

Alissa was tall with electric orange hair. Really, really tall with legs that stretched from the ground to eternity, and an equally long neck. Those were the first things Jacobi noticed when she peeked out the window to size up her visitor. Superlong legs, an ostrich-length neck, and hair that looked like a blaze of fire. Then she noticed the girl's pleasant demeanor. Jacobi couldn't put her finger on it, but something about the Alissa girl seemed welcoming.

"Hey," Jacobi said as politely as she could when she stepped out onto the porch into the hot sun, adjusting her camera around her neck.

"Hi!" Alissa replied, perkier than Jacobi had ever heard a person be. "I'm Alissa. Your next-door neighbor. That's a cool camera. Videographer?"

Jacobi brightened, nodding her head to Alissa's question and zooming in on a splatter of orange-red freckles that dotted her pale face. She had one of the lightest complexions on a black girl that Jacobi had ever seen, making Jacobi wonder about her heritage. Still, Alissa's appearance didn't deter Jacobi from her uppity mood. Malone, a boy she thought was cuter than any other guy who walked the planet, also lived next door. Maybe he was Alissa's brother. She didn't see a resemblance, though. In fact, besides looking like she could glow at night, Alissa reminded Jacobi a lot of herself. Plain. She wasn't ugly enough to be considered ugly, and definitely was not pretty enough to be considered average. She was just there.

As if reading her thoughts, Alissa nodded her head and pointed in the direction of Malone's house. "Yep. I live over there. I'm your other next-door neighbor. Malone's sister, in case you were wondering." She laughed.

Jacobi nodded and laughed with her.

"Anyway, I thought I'd come introduce myself. I would've done it sooner, but I was on punishment." She shrugged. "I got a B in math. You know how it goes. They acted like I wasn't going to be promoted to the eleventh grade because of it."

Jacobi just nodded, noting that Alissa was a year ahead of her in school. No, she didn't know how punishment for getting a B on your report card went. Her parents would've probably thrown her a party if she'd gotten anything above a C-minus, maybe even a D-plus. She'd been a consistent underachiever who'd barely made the grade her whole academic life, and had barely passed the ninth grade. She'd been too busy for school; that's what Shooby had told her.

"So, I hear you're going to the motorcycle show, too, and I thought we could go together."

Jacobi's brows lifted again, and she tilted her head. "How do you know my business?"

"Easy," Alissa said. "Our mothers have been talking. My mom was swapping how-to-keep-your-lawn-green secrets with your mother, in exchange for how-to-make-red-beans-and-rice secrets, and they were figuring out how to get us to be friends, too, I guess. They even talked about sending me to some film school your mom wants you to go to. Boring stuff." She waved her hand. "But I don't mind. I don't deal with many people around here—too bourgeois and stuck-up for me—if you get what I'm saying. And from what my mom tells me, your family's not like that. So, we'll be cool. So you wanna roll? The show should be hot. It always is . . ."

Jacobi stood there holding her purse and her tongue, then stepped off the porch and made her way to the street, listening as Alissa went on with the speed of her words increasing with each step. She didn't let Jacobi get one word in, and had pronounced bourgeois correctly—*boozh-wah*, not *boozh-ee*. She just kept rattling on and on, and Jacobi kind of liked it, since she wasn't much of a talker herself. Around Alissa, she knew she wouldn't have to say much, and that made her comfortable. Until her face cleared and her breasts sprouted, as far as she was concerned, the less she was noticed, the better.

"You know, you dress like you're from the Valley." Alissa continued the one-sided conversation. "It's cute, though. I kinda like the shoes . . ."

"Oh my, not another one! Orphan Annie has a new friend. A friend with a huge camera around her neck," a girl yelled out, pulling Jacobi's attention.

Alissa grabbed Jacobi by the arm, then picked up the pace. They no longer walked, they marched. "Don't look back. If you don't pay them any attention, they'll go away."

Jacobi couldn't help herself. She turned her head, and about twenty feet behind them were a few girls. Ones she knew she could take on, alone if she had to. It wouldn't be easy, but it was possible. She'd bet a dollar to a dime the clique of girls hadn't rumbled before like she'd had to back in Lancaster.

"Don't look," Alissa urged, walking even faster.

"Who're they?" Jacobi asked, out of breath and baffled by the girls' nastiness. It was hard for her to keep up with Alissa's long strides, so she slowed. She wasn't running from anyone.

Alissa pulled her arm, trying to make her keep pace, but Jacobi refused to move. "Only my biggest enemy.

Yummy. The others are her friends. For now. Next month they'll be on her people-to-hate list, too. C'mon, Jacobi. Let's go."

The girls caught up with Jacobi and Alissa, and were now in front of them. They'd moved quicker than Jacobi believed they could, and now Jacobi wasn't too happy about the switch. From the nasty look the head girl wore, coupled with her huge size, Jacobi would have given anything to still be in front of them, moving as fast as she could to reach her destination. Jacobi held her head high despite her nervousness and came face-to-face with the girl, who had to be at least three times Jacobi's weight. The girl's arms were the size of Jacobi's mother's thighs, her hair was all over her head, crusty sleep crumbles were in the corners of her eyes, and she had chalky stuff around her mouth. Even with the distance between them, Jacobi could hear the girl breathe. She snorted when she inhaled, like she was fighting to fill her lungs, and she huffed her exhale like her breath was celebrating escaping her throat. Out of nowhere, the girl took a powdered doughnut out of a box and stuffed it between her lips. In two bites, it was gone. Jacobi didn't have time for this; she had more important things to do, like go meet Shooby and Katydid, but she wasn't a punk. If the girl wanted to get handled, by hook or crook, rock or stick, Jacobi would handle her.

"Oh my, Orphan Annie has a new friend," the girl repeated, referring to Alissa as the redheaded character from the movie. "Now we have a giraffe and a leopard."

Jacobi cringed. She knew the girl was calling her a

leopard because of her acne-marked face. It wasn't her fault her skin was spotted. "Excuse me?" she asked, her attitude flaring. She might be embarrassed by her uneven breasts and dotted skin, but she wasn't a doormat. No one—not even this girl, Yummy—was going to torment or step on her. "Say it again if you don't like breathing. I'm a what, sleaze?"

The girl swallowed her words, rearing back her head in apparent surprise. "I know you didn't—"

Jacobi took her video camera off her neck, then handed it and her purse to Alissa. "I did. And *what*?" She walked close enough to Yummy to smell her breath. "Don't talk about it, be about it. You had so much to say a second ago when you thought I'd cave."

Suddenly, Malone walked up. Jacobi stepped away from her new enemy, and everyone else froze. He was the epitome of gorgeous. Yummy's nasty glare turned into a smile, and Jacobi's attitude melted. Yummy stepped forward a bit, poking out her well-developed chest. It was more than obvious that Malone had her attention, too. And from what Jacobi could tell, he didn't feel the same way.

"Hi . . . uh? Jacobi? Am I saying your name right?" he asked, looking at Jacobi through sparkling baby-browns. His eyes were the prettiest she'd ever seen on a boy, and his lashes were long enough to put mascara-wearers to shame. "Nice camera." His compliment showed he was impressed, and his traveling gaze said he was sizing her up.

Jacobi just stared at him, taking him in one blink at a

time. He was almost as tall as Diggs. Over six-one, he had short, rich caramel-brown hair. It was cut close, but not too short to hide his God-given curls. In fact, up close, Malone was so perfectly breathtaking that she couldn't say anything. Nothing. Not even one word would come out of her mouth. She just knew he looked better than any of the girls surrounding him, and that upped her crush that bordered on stalking. Their bathroom window faced his, and there were times she couldn't help but watch him. He'd primp like a girl, but, from a distance, she noted, there was nothing feminine about him. He had a routine she liked to follow. First, she'd watch him do shirtless push-ups in his bedroom, then her eyes followed him to the dresser mirror, where she'd admire him fixing his hair. After that, she'd daydream about them being a couple as she watched him change clothes, while feelings moved through her body that she didn't understand. Then he'd leave his room, and, like a feign, she'd run to the living room window to drool at him as he backed out of the driveway in one of his parents' cars. No, she wouldn't be watching him anymore because she was crushing on him. She'd keep an eye on him to see if he was filmable. Boys just weren't supposed to be delicious. Cute—like Shooby—was good. Over-the-top fine like Malone was a killer to a girl's ego. He just looked like he'd want nothing to do with someone who looked like her.

Alissa elbowed her in the ribs and cleared her throat.

"Yes. Yes. I'm Jacobi," she managed to say, then flashed Alissa a thank-you smile.

Malone nodded. "Cool. I thought so. Can you take my

number and give it to your brother, and tell Diggs to hit me later?"

Sure she would take his number, and him, too, if she wasn't with Shooby. Well, she wasn't Shooby's girl yet. And *yet* was the operative word.

"*Diggs?* Diggs is *your* brother?" Yummy asked, her eyes now wide and interested. "I didn't know you were Diggs's sister. You should've said so. That changes everything."

Jacobi threw Yummy a nasty sideways look and dismissed her with an eye roll. She reached into her purse to get her phone, but couldn't find it. She grimaced. How could she have come out of the house without it? Not when she needed it most, and definitely not when she'd relied on it to hear from Shooby and their flash-mob updates. "I must've left my cell at home. Sorry."

Malone smiled. "No problem. I do it all the time. But if you don't mind—" He patted his front pockets, then retrieved his wallet from the back one. He fished out a business card and handed it to Jacobi. "I don't normally give these out, but I really need to talk to Diggs. You'd really be doing me a huge favor if you give that to him."

"There's something I'd like to give him, too," Yummy said.

Jacobi shot the girl a glare, then turned back to Malone and smiled. "I'll give it to him later. He's not at home."

"Thanks," he said, winking. "Are you going to the motorcycle show?"

"Yes," Jacobi and Alissa said in unison.

"I want to see what I can capture on film . . . well, digitally," she admitted, then wanted to kick herself for allowing her enthusiasm to rise. She was such a nerd, and it showed.

He shot a weird look at Alissa, then pressed his lips together like he was trying to decide something. He shrugged, turned back to Jacobi, and smiled. "Cool. Real cool. I like that you're so passionate. Anyway, I'm headed to the motorcycle show, too, so we can go together," he offered, surprising everyone. "And I guess"—he nodded toward Alissa—"you can come, too."

# 4

# KASSIDY

There was no way she was going to deal with the mess. Not Los Angeles. Not her new neighborhood. Definitely not her new evil stepsister. "Uh-uh, no way," Kassidy said, slamming the screen door behind her and adjusting the sunglasses she religiously wore while in the sun. She jogged down the few porch steps and bent over to tighten her laces. She needed to get in the wind to stay fit and clear her mind. She had no idea how she was going to adjust to the move, and had to figure a way out. Literally. She could call her dad, but he was across the ocean conducting business in China, and her grandmother lived back in New York in a one-bedroom condo in a senior building. So for either of them to save her was out of the question. But she was sure there had to be a way. She was going to get back to the city that never slept and her boyfriend, Brent. She'd been trying to contact him since last night, but for some reason his phone had been disconnected. She'd tried again this morning, nine times, and still no success. Desperate, she'd texted his address to Faith, offering to pay her to go see him, and, hopefully, by now she'd contacted him. Until she heard back, she had to find a way to not think about him. Her only tried and true solution was connecting her feet with the concrete for as long and fast as she could run.

"Hey, beautiful," a male voice greeted from behind.

Kassidy rolled her eyes. *Ugh.* It would be like a boy to catcall her while she was bent over. All they ever thought about was getting an eyeful, and she would know; she'd dealt with boys peeking behind the drawn curtains at runway shows while she and the other models dressed.

"Whoever you are, what do you want?" she asked, still tightening her laces.

"Just thought I'd welcome you to the neighborhood," he said. "Because you have to be new here. If you weren't, I'd know. I'd never forget a pretty face like yours."

"You can't even see my face. So try again," she said, standing up and turning to look at him. What her eyes saw was pretty tempting and definitely worth her time, but a little young for her taste. He stood straddling a large silver moped and wearing a smile. His skin was sun kissed, and his wavy hair gleamed like shiny wax. She nodded. If he wasn't good for anything else, he could prove to be the distraction she needed while missing Brent and her life in Manhattan, she decided. The fact that he had wheels—even if only two of them—was a definite plus, though she knew her hair would get messed up. "Next time you want to get a girl's attention"—she took off her shades and looked him in the eyes—"talk to her face, not her butt," she deadpanned.

His smile widened. "The view was great, so I couldn't help it. But I apologize. I'm Romero."

"Okay, for the apology," she teased, flirting. "I'm Kassidy," she said, standing tall. The run could wait, and so could saving her hairdo. Right now she needed to go, zoom away, find something to do until Faith gave her a heads-up on Brent's happenings and whereabouts, and literally let it all blow in the wind—her hair and her attitude. "And if you're really sorry, you could take me somewhere. Anywhere."

Romero nodded, gripped the hand brakes, and revved the moped's motor a bit. "Okay, take the helmet off the back and hop on. You are new around here, right? How old are you?"

Kassidy had the helmet on her head and her sunglasses back on before she knew it. "Right, I'm new. I'm fifteen. You?" she asked, hopping on behind him. Wrapping her arms around his waist, she held on, ready to ride.

"Fifteen, too. That's why I'm whipping a moped. Gotta be sixteen for a real motorcycle." He laughed. "I would ask you where you want to go, but since you're new around here, you don't know," he said, looking over his shoulder.

"But I do know where I want to go." Kassidy smiled, then purposely bit her lip. She'd read somewhere that the move was flirtatious and guys found it attractive, so she did it, and it worked. "I want you to take me everywhere."

"Cool. But what will your boyfriend say?" he asked, clearly wanting to know if she had one.

Kassidy smirked, tightening the chinstrap on the helmet. She winked. "Probably the same thing your girlfriend will say. So, are we going to ride, or talk about things like boyfriends and girlfriends—people who aren't really a part of this conversation? I didn't ask if you had one, so I obviously don't care. You don't really care if I have a boyfriend, either. If so, you'd have asked before inviting me out."

The intersection of North La Brea and Centinela Avenues boasted three things Kassidy needed: drink, food, and boys, in that order. The high-end coffee shop they were parked in front of was known for its many caffeine specialties, but also served her favorite, green tea. Her eyes flashed across the parking lot, to the right. There stood a T.G.I. Friday's, and it was super busy, reminding her she hadn't eaten all day. She smiled, her day getting better by the glance. A group of guys on real motorcycles were gathered in front of it.

Romero killed the engine and hopped off the moped. "You coming?" he asked, holding out his hand to help her off.

Kassidy forced her attention away from the gathering of boys and smiled at Romero. "No, I think I'll just stay out here, if you don't mind. I'll keep your seat warm . . . and maybe stretch my legs," she said, taking out her phone to check if Faith had texted yet.

He nodded. "No problem. It can get a little tight riding

on the back. What do you want to drink? There are like a million types of coffee in there."

"I like tea. And since you talked to me, I'm sure you have good taste." She winked. "Surprise me."

Before the coffee shop door closed behind Romero, Kassidy was up and off the moped and headed toward the restaurant. Even in running gear, she knew she looked great. She wasn't catwalk ready, but being a model had given her an air of superiority and a confidence many didn't have, and she used hers to her advantage. Every day. Being confident was one of her strong points, and was the thing that had snagged Brent's attention, making him choose her over other girls. Being a male model himself, he'd had a lot of claws digging into him, but hers had been the sharpest, and she'd pulled him in without a problem. And today, she noted, sashaying as she walked, there wouldn't be any problems getting California dudes, either. All eyes were on her when she passed the group of guys. She slyly eyed them back. She didn't want to waste her time by talking to the first one who spoke; she needed to shop and scope out one worthy of her attention.

"Hello," she said, nodding and scanning the group as she walked by. Happily, she'd noticed one or two out of the bunch who were cute, but she still wasn't quite sure who would be worthy. Whoever he was had to be a leader, superfine, and the one everyone else in the group wanted to imitate. She knew she had to give it another shot. All she needed was one more look to know.

She stopped and patted her pockets when she was a

few yards away from them. She shook her head and huffed loud enough for them to hear.

"You okay? Lose something?" one of them asked, taking her bait.

Kassidy turned around and walked toward the guys. Carefully, she scanned their faces, and, sure enough, there were two extracute ones. But gorgeous wasn't enough. She needed to know who had the swagger to match his looks.

One of the supercute guys hopped off his motorcycle, then strode to her. The others followed. Kassidy nodded. He had to be the one because he was definitely the leader, and he was definitely gorgeous.

"You okay? Lose something? 'Cause I can help you find it . . . if you like."

Kassidy consumed him with a blink of her eye. She was a pro at the quick sweep—glancing fast, but still seeing if a boy was cute. And that he was. "My key ring. There's only one key on it, so it could've dropped without my noticing. It has my name on it—Kassidy, with a *K*. So you can't miss it or mistake it," she said, offering him her name on the sly.

He nodded and smiled, showing off deep dimples and a cleft chin. He wore braids, usually a no-no for her, but they looked good on him. "Okay, Ms. New York, Kassidy with a *K*. I'm Carsen, with a *C*. I recognize your accent. It's cute like you." He licked his lips. "Let's go find your key." He offered Kassidy his hand and led the way, backtracking the way she'd walked. "Hey, help me find Ms. New York's key," he said to the guys.

Like clockwork all eyes were on the ground, and Kassidy stood to the side while Carsen's flunkies did the work. Her eyes bounced between the coffee shop, looking for Romero, and Carsen. She didn't know how she was going to pull off juggling both guys, but she would. Of that she was certain. There was no way she was giving up on either of her new options.

"So, Kassidy? I seen you ride up with someone else— but I'm not worried about him, though. I'm not a hater, I'm a participator. So you think I can call you?"

She really smiled then. Carsen was just what she needed. A boy who knew how to play her game. She waved her hand. "Stop it! I'm so not his girlfriend. If I was, I wouldn't be talking to you. That's just my boy. He gave me a ride . . . we're looking for my stepsister—his *girlfriend*. So, it's cool. And yes, you can call me, maybe even take me out later. Lock in my number."

She rattled off her digits while he entered them into his phone, then gave him her phone so he could enter his number. Then she somehow managed to "accidentally" locate her key in her pocket. With apologies for wasting Carsen's and his friends' time, she headed back to the coffee shop to meet Romero just as he was coming outside.

"Aw, thank you," she said when she saw the large cups he carried. "I just know you picked my fave. Let's drink up so we can roll out. I can't wait to see the rest of Los Angeles!" She took her seat on the back of the moped.

Romero handed her a cold cup, then rubbed his hand over his hair. He smiled. "I had them ice your tea. It's too hot for hot tea. And Los Angeles is pretty big. Seeing it all can take days, weeks even."

Her phone vibrated, and she looked at it. Again, it was an unknown caller. Kassidy ignored the call, then cheesed at Romero. Thanks to her mom moving them to LA, she had time. She had days and weeks; months, too. That is, if she couldn't get back to New York and Brent. Until then, she couldn't think of a better way to make the transition easier and more fun than to have a boy or two help her out. "If you have time, I certainly do. My days are free," she offered. *Because my nights will be spent with Carsen or whoever the next lucky contestant is,* she thought.

# 5

## JACOBI

Malone was the dude. THE DUDE in all caps, Jacobi decided. She'd walked as close to him as she could, inhaling his masculine scent and nodding her head while trying to stay undetected. He'd wooed her with his coolness and easy conversation, and didn't mind stopping by her house so she could get her phone. Pretty or not, she couldn't shake the comfortable feeling he'd given her, and he felt more to her like a brother or friend than anything. She craned her neck, looking in the direction she thought they should go. The bus stop was down the street and around the corner—at least she thought it was until they hung a left. She looked over at Alissa, who shrugged, then proved herself bold.

"Hey, Malone? Where're we going? Aren't you taking Dad's car?" Alissa asked, running her hand through her shock of red hair.

Malone stopped in his tracks and huffed. He put his

hands in his pockets. "I . . ." He paused and pressed his lips together like he was stopping himself from saying something. "*Me and Jacobi* are riding to the bike show. I'm taking *her* in *my* whip, not Dad's. And, because you're with *her*, you get to go. Don't forget that you snitched on me last week."

Jacobi looked from Malone to Alissa, wondering what Alissa had told. Alissa didn't respond with words. Her face said it all. And her expression said *defeated*. Eyes focused on the ground, Alissa acted as if her head was too heavy to lift. Her lips were pursed together, and she rolled her eyes.

*Brother and sister mess.* Jacobi elbowed her lightly. "You cool?" she whispered, genuinely concerned but also excited. She tried to contain the exuberant, confusing energy racing inside her. Minutes ago, she'd demoted Malone to just a pretty guy who'd never compare to Shooby, and now she was more than happy to be riding anywhere with Malone. Still, she didn't like him *like him*. That's the lie she told herself. But having someone else to talk to was tempting. Plus, now that she knew he and Alissa had a problem, she was sure she'd be riding up front next to him, which would give her a chance to see what he was really about. There had to be more to him than just looks.

Alissa nodded, then swallowed hard enough for Jacobi to see a lump rise in her throat. "I'm good," she said with obviously false perkiness. "He just gets on my nerves."

Jacobi shrugged. She hadn't known Alissa long enough to know how to read her, and she didn't want to get involved in whatever drama Alissa and Malone had. All she was interested in was Malone, getting to the motorcycle show to see if Katydid was there, and hooking up with Shooby afterward. Well, those things, of course, and solving her physical problems. Namely, her bad skin and underdevelopment. "Okay."

They'd turned the corner, crossed a couple of lawns, and were headed to a garage before Jacobi knew it. From what she could tell from his spat with his sister, Malone had his own car. She had never seen his ride before and really hadn't even known he had one.

"This is it," Malone said, cutting across the lawn of a large white stucco house. He took a remote and a set of keys out of his pocket. He pressed a button when he turned, then walked to the side of the house and up the drive.

"Wow, that's tight," Jacobi said, following him and admiring the car that had to have cost three arms and four legs. She was no vehicle enthusiast, but knew from television that this was a car that pro ballplayers and other rich people drove; and a couple of doughboys from the projects had one. "This is *yours*?"

Malone turned and smiled, walking to the luxury car parked in the oversized garage. He nodded. "Yep. Bought and paid for by yours truly. I keep it over here at my grandpop's house because he has room in his garage."

Jacobi turned to the hesitant and lagging-behind Alissa. Jacobi's expression asked her if he was serious.

Alissa nodded, gave her a where've-you-been look, then threw up her hands in exasperation. "Did you look at the business card he gave you?" she whispered, incredulous.

Trying to be as inconspicuous as she could, Jacobi pretended to search for something in her purse as she looked at his card. *Wow.* Malone's card was no ordinary business card. It was more of a mini-résumé. He was an actor and model who'd been on a couple of sitcoms and in various major magazines. *Wow again.* She stomped the concrete in anticipation. If only he'd let her film him, it could be the start of her film career.

"You okay?" Malone asked, stopping by the trunk.

Jacobi smiled, still stomping. "Yeah," she lied. "Just a few red ants, but I'm cool."

He walked over to her, took her by the arm, and led her to the passenger side of his car. Surprising Jacobi, he opened the door for her and helped her into the car. "They can't get you while you're inside. Strap in. I wouldn't want anything to happen to you." He winked, closed the door, then went around to the driver's side and settled inside behind the wheel. He started the car and revved the engine. "And I hope you don't have a boyfriend . . ."

*Oh God. Did he just say what I heard him say?* Jacobi wondered, then turned toward the backseat where Alissa was sliding in, and shot her a questioning look.

Alissa shook her head in the negative, mouthing, "Say no. Say no."

"No!" Jacobi said a little too loudly. "Not really," she continued in a more appropriate voice, making Malone, who was still talking, pause and smile. Her answer also made her think. No, she really didn't have a true love interest who was also interested in her, and the thought didn't make her feel too good. It made her determined to go out there and get Shooby. She needed to turn the negative into a positive. And if Katydid was able to make it to the motorcycle show like she'd said she'd try to, Jacobi had a chance of finally making it happen. Katydid had promised to help.

" 'Cause I'm letting the top down, you know," he began again, pressing a button then backing out of the driveway. "And if you had a boyfriend—which you said you don't, right?"—he licked his lips, putting the car in Drive, then accelerating down the street—"then I wouldn't want you to get into trouble. But since you don't have a boyfriend—which you said, right?"—he licked his lips once more and hung the corner—"we have nothing to worry about."

Jacobi looked at him and her lips spread into a wide smile, showing off the metal tracks across her teeth. *Oh, but if I could have a boyfriend, it'd be you*, she thought but said, "No, we don't have nothing to worry—"

"Oh no. Oh God, no," Alissa yelled from the backseat, interrupting and startling Jacobi and Malone. "Stop the car. Stop the car. Please."

Jacobi jerked forward when Malone stomped on the breaks. "What's wrong?"

"What is it now, Alissa?" Malone yelled.

"Just take me home," Alissa pleaded hysterically. "Please just take me and Jacobi to the house. It's an emergency. A girl emergency." Tears sprang from Alissa's eyes, and she wiped them away as fast as they came.

Jacobi stared at Alissa, trying to read her face behind the tears. She wanted to comfort her, to help her, but all she could do was say "Oh" when she found out what Alissa's emergency was.

"My period. My period just came," Alissa mouthed.

*Dang. I still haven't got mine. No pretty skin. No straight teeth. No boobs. And no period, either.* "Dear God," she prayed under her breath, "I know I said I was through asking for things, but I really need you to do me another favor . . ."

# 6

# KASSIDY

She knew it was super late. Hours ago, when the sun set and the stars lit, Kassidy knew that what her mother would've considered too late for her to be out of the house had passed. Now too late had turned into early. Like early enough to get in trouble because it had to be past midnight, which meant it was beyond three in the morning in New York—way past Brent's bedtime. She shrugged. It really didn't matter at this point because Brent's phone was still off, and Faith had texted that she couldn't find him. Kassidy shook her head and unwound her arms from Romero's waist. She wasn't happy. She was sore about her missing-in-action boyfriend, and hated to leave Romero and face her new life. It wasn't because she liked Romero; it was because she had no choice. She may've earned her own money since she was ten, but she still wasn't grown, although she'd felt like an adult since she'd taken on the responsibility of a career.

Kassidy looked at her watch, and, sure enough, she was right. It was almost one thirty in the morning, and would be well past that when she snuck into the house.

"Hate that you gotta go," Romero said, hopping off the moped to help her off.

Kassidy smiled. She hated to leave him as much as he wanted her to stay. They'd had a ball, and he'd been such a sweetheart. He'd taken her to a couple of beaches, a local burger joint that had the best cheeseburgers on the planet, and even a real taco stand. They'd walked, talked, and Kassidy really liked Romero—as a friend, with the possibility of one day becoming more. But today wasn't the day he'd climb her more-than-friends ladder, and he wouldn't be here when the sun rose, either. She had big plans. Ones that included going with Carsen to the last day of the motorcycle show. After she awoke, she was his for the entire day; that's what she'd promised him via text when Romero wasn't looking.

Kassidy stretched and yawned, then looked around the neighborhood. Despite the adults having to work in the morning, a few teenagers were still out. She nodded. Her home in the Hills was looking a little better each minute, especially now that she realized she wasn't the only one around with a late-night pulse. It still wasn't New York, but it was starting to appear doable.

"So . . . ?" Romero said, walking up to her. "Can I at least get a good-bye hug?"

Kassidy pursed her lips, then glanced sideways. She knew what Romero was up to, and she wasn't kissing him. Uh-uh and no way. She would flirt, hang out, and make promises, but that was it. Her lips were reserved for Brent alone. "Sure," she said, and reached for him. She stretched her arms as far as she could, making sure to keep as much distance as possible between her body and his, then hugged him like a brother. "Thanks for today. I really appreciate it," she said, letting him go and stepping back.

Romero nodded, then laughed as smoothly and coolly as a guy could after he'd been sort of rejected. "No problem. So . . . tomorrow?"

Kassidy shook her head, feigning a look of disappointment. "I have to finish unpacking, then it's family day. Maybe the day after?" she asked. She blew him an air kiss while walking backward, then she turned to hightail it home to climb through the first available unlocked window she could find.

She'd almost worked her way around the entire house before she found a cracked window. Kassidy shook her head and took a deep breath. She hadn't been there long enough to be sure which room she was sneaking into, but wherever it was, it wasn't the one she'd have chosen if she'd had a choice. Soft lights showed through the blinds, and she was sure she could hear a faint sound inside. She wasn't sure if it was a television or music, but the noise was a constant drone.

Wiping her hands on her clothes, she dried the nervous sweat from her palms and stepped back to survey the distance from the ground. The bottom of the window had to be at least five feet up from where she stood. "Whew!" she exhaled, glad that she was taller than average. Carefully pressing her hands on the frame, she leaned her weight into the wooden frame and awkwardly pushed in and up. She'd learned long ago that if she pressed hard on window frames and floors, less noise would be made. It was the squeaking and creaking that alerted parents that something was going on.

With relative ease and almost complete silence, the window rose. Kassidy reached over and gripped the bottom of the sill with all her might, then pulled herself up by her arms and walked her feet up the side of the house until her head pushed through the blinds. A television screen met her eyes and a loud scream sounded in her ears. *Dang.* She was in Yummy's room. She would've kicked herself for forgetting the layout of the house, but she hadn't been there long enough to memorize it.

"Help. Help! Someone's breaking in!" Yummy yelled.

Kassidy, halfway in and hanging over the window frame, looked right at her new stepsister, trying to shush her.

"Yeah, right," Yummy said, rolling her eyes. She began screaming like someone was killing her. "Help!"

Still in the awkward position, Kassidy's heart dropped to her midsection when her mother and stepfather ran inside the room and caught her sneaking in.

"Help!" Yummy screamed louder, hopping in place and shielding her eyes with her arms.

Kassidy just looked at her, sure that Yummy had covered her eyes in an attempt to fool their parents into believing that she didn't see Kassidy. "Enough already!" Kassidy hissed. She sneered at her stepsister. "You know it's me. Don't act like you don't."

"Kassidy!" her mother cried out, walking toward the

window. "What are you doing sneaking in here at this time of night, scaring everyone?" She grabbed Kassidy by her arms and pulled her through. "Get in here. Now!" she said, as if Kassidy had a choice.

Disgusted with Yummy, Kassidy rolled her eyes again.

"I know you didn't just roll your eyes at me!" her mother hissed, then grabbed Kassidy by her bicep and began pulling her toward the door. "I can give you something to roll your eyes at."

Kassidy planted her feet firmly on the floor and pulled away from her mom. "I didn't roll my eyes at you. I'm rolling my eyes at *her* and her antics. Can anyone say drama queen?"

"Okay, babe. I see you can handle this. I'm going back to bed now," her stepfather said, wearing a confused look and shaking his head. "Call me if you need me."

"G'night," Kassidy said to him. "Sorry I woke you, but I wasn't sneaking in—"

"Yes, you were." Her mom cut her off, pointing toward the door. "Now get in your room. You and I have some talking to do."

Kassidy stomped toward the door, then shot Yummy the nastiest look she could. "I'm going to get you," she threatened as she walked out.

She turned right once she was in the hall, but her mother guided her in the opposite direction. Kassidy shrugged. How was she supposed to remember where her room was, after living here for less than twenty-four hours—and in the dark, at that?

"Mom? Please. I wasn't sneaking in. I was locked

out—Yummy locked me out on purpose." She continued to lie while walking to her room, then went inside.

Her mother's brows shifted from extremely low—a clear sign that she was upset—to the ceiling—a giveaway that she was curious. "Really?" she said, closing the door behind them. "Locked you out from where? *Here?* Home? Where you should've been hours ago?"

Kassidy held her eyes open for what seemed like a small eternity. She knew if she didn't blink they'd water and teardrops would fall. A couple of them, anyway. And that's all she needed—to look like she was crying. After her eyes burned from lack of moisture, two drops ran down her cheeks, gaining her the sympathy she needed. "Mom, I was just outside with Faith. She got back from New York earlier and came by. We were on the porch discussing agencies—I don't know if I should switch or not. You know, I need to make myself a brand," she said, throwing up her hands. She knew shoptalk would always get to her mom. Her mother was her manager, so she was doubly protective. "Why don't you look out the window? Plenty of kids are still out, and Faith and I were with them. Not really *with them* with them, but we were all hanging outside—I was still home. Look and see," she lied, thinking she'd have to put Faith up on the untruth she'd told. She knew her mom would double-check.

Her mother's icy look melted when she looked through the blinds. "Okay, Kass. But just so you learn your lesson, you have to stay around here today. You can't just go around not coming in and not asking permission. How was I supposed to know you were out front?"

Kassidy's heart fell to her midsection again. She was supposed to see Carsen later, and now, because of her evil stepsister, that wasn't going to happen. Hate wasn't a strong enough word for what she felt for Yummy, and she could think of only one that was: revenge. And that's exactly what she planned for her stepsister.

# 7

# *JACOBI*

Her head was throbbing. Really banging. Ever since Malone had dropped them off, all she could do was think about getting to Shooby and the motorcycle show and her first real date. That's the only way she could describe her expectations for her time together with Shooby: a date. She liked to think that Shooby would treat her the same way Malone had treated her. Malone had complimented her, held open the car door, and flirted: all the things she believed a guy would do when taking a girl out. *So, why not?* she thought, shrugging. Why shouldn't she see her time with Malone as a hint of what she should expect from Shooby? Someone treating her special, like Malone had done. But for some reason, she knew Shooby wouldn't. She rolled her eyes as tension climbed her neck. The same tightness that'd made Jacobi's headache kick in as soon as Alissa had insisted on going home, thereby killing the idea of her meeting up with Shooby.

"You okay in there?" Jacobi yelled as she sat on the floor next to the bathroom door, texting Shooby that she was running late and simultaneously mentally practicing *to the East. To the West* . . . Her eyes were on her breasts, then she looked up and around in awe. Alissa didn't have a bedroom; she had a suite, complete with her own sitting area and bathroom. She guessed that's what living closer to the top of the hill offered: teenage suites. Where she lived—one house closer to the bottom of the hill—teenagers like her and Diggs shared a bathroom with little five-year-olds named Hunter. It was amazing that living one house down could really make a difference in floor plans.

"No. I need you. Come in," Alissa replied.

What, exactly, was she supposed to do in the bathroom? Jacobi wondered. Especially when Alissa was having girl problems. "A friend in need . . ." she said, reminding herself of her manners and pushing herself up from the floor. Reluctantly, she twisted the knob and opened the door, then popped her head inside. To her relief, Alissa was sitting behind a four-foot-high frosted glass partition, and all Jacobi could see were Alissa's mile-long legs sticking out. "Yeah?"

"Can you look in the cabinet under the sink and hand me a pad? A regular one," Alissa explained, reaching her hand over the partition.

Jacobi nodded as if Alissa could see her, then looked in the cabinet and almost choked. Feminine products in various colors and sizes were stacked high, and she couldn't differentiate one from the other. Sure, she could tell the douche from the pads and the pads from the vaginal washes, but she had no idea how to determine a "regular" pad from the others; and none were in boxes, just neatly stacked in a rattan basket. As she stared at the variety of girl stuff, she realized she didn't even know exactly what the douche and feminine wash were for. Sure, she knew the region of the body the products were made for, but she couldn't explain why and when they were needed. She gritted her teeth in frustration at her ignorance. Altogether there were six pads: a trio of pinks, two yellows, and a white one. She decided to try one of the pads wrapped in pink plastic. "Here," she said, taking it from the cabinet and walking over to hand it to Alissa.

"Uh-uh," Alissa said after she took it and examined it. "I'm not that heavy." She handed it back to Jacobi.

Jacobi quietly breathed out her frustration as she headed back to the cabinet. She didn't want Alissa to know she knew nothing about pads, so she couldn't just ask what color she needed. "I really need to get to the show, Alissa. No offense." Quickly looking at the pad in her hand, she sized it up, then selected a smaller one. "I hope this is it," she said, accidentally voicing her thoughts, then cringing when she realized it was too late.

"Are you kidding me?" Alissa asked from behind the partition.

"No. My best friend from my old neighborhood, Katy-did, might come. And I'm supposed to meet another friend there. It's kinda important." An eye roll punctuated the last word. "I don't mean to be rude."

"No, not that. I'm talking about pads. You don't know about pads? Oh my God, Jacobi! That can only mean one thing . . ." Alissa was quiet for a moment, reaching farther over the frosted glass. "You haven't had your period yet?"

Jacobi rolled her eyes again, making her way over with her second pad selection, handing the plastic-wrapped feminine product to Alissa. She shook her head, then remembered Alissa couldn't see her, and she was glad. She didn't want her new friend to see the embarrassment on her face. "Not yet," she admitted, perkier than she felt.

"Hmm," Alissa said from behind the partition, noisily unwrapping the pad. "I wonder why."

"Why?" There has to be a why? Jacobi worried. Was there something wrong with her? Maybe her female organs were off.

Alissa appeared from behind the partition, then walked to the sink and washed her hands. She looked at Jacobi in the mirror and shrugged. "Are you anorexic or bulimic or something? You know that'll throw your system off and your period will *never* come. I went to school with this girl who made herself throw up." She turned around and leaned against the sink, crossing her arms as if accusing Jacobi of having an eating disorder. "You know you can talk to me if you do. My mom's a nutritionist, so that makes me a nutritionist in training. Food can do all kinds of screwy things to your body. Trust me."

Jacobi tsk-tsked her and vehemently shook her head. She didn't have an eating disorder. If anything, she needed to slow down on her eating habits because she consumed too much sugar; that's what the pimples on her face told her, though she didn't indulge in too many sweets. The sugar had to be coming from somewhere. *Maybe too much fruit?* "Are you crazy? I don't know why I haven't had my period yet, but I know it's not because of an eating disorder. I eat. I eat all the time, and I don't throw up."

Alissa stared at Jacobi for seconds, pursing her lips together. She bent down, opened the cabinet Jacobi had been in, fished inside for a while, and stood up with a handful of maxi pads. "I got my period when I was eleven, and everyone else I know had theirs by thirteen at the latest. So that means your hormones are off. That's your problem. It's probably the reason your chest is almost concave, too—your breasts are growing *in*to your chest instead of out of it. We may need to research your symptoms. But first, I need to give you a lesson in feminine products."

Jacobi's eyes lit. She'd never had a lesson on pads other than during the sex ed classes she had to take in sixth and seventh grades. Heaven forbid her mother should talk to her about such a thing; that was much too taboo for her. Her parents' generation seemed allergic to discussing stuff like sex, anatomy, and menstrual cycles.

"Alissa," a guy's voice called from outside the bathroom door, followed by a loud knock. "Phone! Your cell phone's been buzzing nonstop, and if you don't come get it, it's going in the trash. And weren't you supposed to be at your piano lesson today? Mom told me to make sure you got there, or else we both are gonna be in trouble. And I ain't taking the heat for nobody. You better hurry or I'm telling," he threatened.

Jacobi raised her brows at Alissa.

Rolling her eyes, Alissa kicked the cabinet door closed and handed Jacobi the armful of maxi pads. "Okay. Okay," she said to the door, then turned to Jacobi. "Here. Take these home and study them. I forgot I have this stupid lesson today. So it's probably a good thing we missed the motorcycle show, or I'd definitely be in major trouble. But there's always tomorrow, right?" She threw a sideways glance at the door. "Oh, and that pain in the ya-know out there is Alek, better known as my twin brother. You can ignore him on your way out. Oh, yeah . . ." She trailed off as she bent down and fished in the cabinet again. "Take these, too. They're stickups, better known as tampons," she said, standing up and thrusting more girly products at Jacobi. "But you want to research those before you try them. Lots of them have chlorine in them, and they can cause your body to go into shock, which is why I have so many. No way I'm using those."

Jacobi's back was to Alissa's front porch before she knew it. Her purse, almost bursting from all the sanitary products, banged against her leg as she jogged down the few stairs to the sidewalk. She had to get home, drop off the bundle of period stuff, then skate as fast as she could to the motorcycle show. Shooby had sent her a hurry-up-or-else message.

"Hey! Where are you going? What did you take?" Alek's voice boomed from behind her.

Jacobi turned and froze, trying to make out Alek's expression through the dark screen door. First she'd been accused of having an eating disorder, and now theft. She scowled. "What's up with this family?" she mumbled under her breath, then put her hands on her hips. She turned easily into her old self—the rough girl she was forced to be in her old neighborhood—snaking her neck and rolling her eyes. She spat, "You must be trippin'! I'm no thief. I didn't take—"

"I'm just playing," he said, stepping out onto the porch, waving his hand and smiling. "I was just trying to stop you from running out of here before I got a chance to introduce myself." He stepped off the porch, walking toward her and offering her his hand like a businessman. "I'm Alek. You are?"

Jacobi took him in with each step. The closer he got to her, the more intently she stared. Alek was also sort of cute. He wasn't rough-and-rugged fine like Shooby, and definitely wasn't typical Hollywood and made-for-TV dreamy like Malone, but, to his credit, he was a semi head-turner. He was just straight attractive in a can't-take-just-one-look way. Upon closer inspection, she realized he wasn't just appealing, he was downright exotic. His eyes were almond shaped and the clearest emerald green she'd ever seen. He had brand-new-baby smooth skin that looked like he'd bathed in milk and honey. And his hair, an inch or two too long, was wild and reddish caramel brown, a toned-down version of Alissa's. Jacobi was sure that his do was the definition of "bed head" that she'd been trying to figure out for a couple of years. And, oh God, was it sexy. More appropriate, she thought *he* was sexy—then she could've kicked herself for emotionally cheating on Shooby and eyeing both Alissa's brothers. "Uh," she stammered as he approached and stood in front of her, forcing her to look up. Way up. He had to be at least six-foot-four. He smiled pleasantly, and she zoomed in. Braces were wrapped around his teeth. Not silver ones like hers, but, sure enough, they were there and not as clear as they were advertised to be. "I'm Jacobi. I live next—"

"Door. I know. I've seen you come and go. Diggs is your brother," he said, still smiling and making her heart soar at his categorization of her. Everyone else she knew thought of her as Diggs's sister—making her brother seem more important. But for Alek it was the other way around. "How old are you?" Alek asked, stepping closer and leaving less than two feet between them.

Jacobi swallowed, sure that he could hear the gulp she'd just forced down her throat. "I'm almost sixteen," she said, because being almost sixteen sounded way better and more mature than fifteen.

He nodded, still smiling, then reached toward her chest.

"Hey!" she responded, jumping back and swatting his hand.

Alek, ignoring the slap, gently pulled her video camera toward him and inspected it. "Hey, what?" He laughed and looked into her eyes. "Oh, you thought I was trying to touch your . . . ?"

Embarrassed, Jacobi shook her head, blushing. "Sorry for hitting you."

Alek shrugged. ". . . Camera," he said, switching nouns on her and ignoring her apology. "Well, you can't blame me. It is very nice *equipment* you have. Not too big. Not too small. Perfect." He winked.

Jacobi's whole world rocked with the blink of his eye.

She couldn't believe he was flirting with her and actually said her breasts were perfect. He hadn't used the exact words, but they both knew he wasn't referring to her camera. Shaking her head, she was sure he was partially blind. If not, what else could be the excuse for his not seeing that one of her boobs was darn near deflated?

"So, Jacobi. You got a man?"

Jacobi shook her head in the negative, revealing her status while reminding herself that Shooby hadn't been interested enough to step up and claim her as his own yet.

"Good. Pass me your phone."

Jacobi looked at Alek's hand and saw that he had a phone. "Why do you need it when you already have one?"

"I *want* to erase all your male contacts." He laughed. "No, but serious. I need to put my number in, in case you ever decide you *need* me," he said, starting to close up the twenty-four-plus inches between them, then stopping abruptly. His beautiful smile died. "Dang," he whispered, looking toward the street, sheer disgust now on his face.

"What's wrong?" Jacobi asked, sorry he'd stopped. Sure, she liked Shooby, but there was something interesting about Alek, especially his bluntness and forwardness about wanting her to call him. But she didn't like him. Not at all. Like his brother, he was worthy of being filmed. But Malone had captured her attention more than that. He was worth getting to know. If she had to choose between the brothers—which she didn't, she told herself—her choice would be Malone.

Alek licked his lips, clearly thinking. "On second thought," he began, reaching around to his back pocket. "Here." A pen appeared in his hand, and then he took her hand. Like they were third graders, he wrote on her palm. "Take care of that, and use it. Anytime."

Jacobi looked at her palm and smiled. His number was written in black ink in large letters.

"Hey, you! Diggs's sister?" a loud female voice asked from behind them.

Jacobi turned and the world crashed under the weight of the last person she wanted to see. "Uh . . ."

"Yummy, remember?" she asked, smacking. "Your new best friend." She turned her attention to Alek. "Hey, white boy!" she sang, clearly flirting. "You know you pushing up on your brother Malone's girl, right?" She winked at Jacobi.

Jacobi turned back to look at Alek and shrugged her shoulders. She didn't know what Yummy was talking about. She turned back to the snacking troublemaker. "Malone's what? I was only riding—"

"I thought you said you didn't have a boyfriend," Alek said, cutting her off. Confusion covered his face.

Jacobi laughed and turned to face him. She didn't know what else to do. "I don't."

"So you're not messing with Malone?" Alek asked, his question more of a statement than a query.

Yummy's laugh rumbled from behind, followed by a faint mechanical purr that pulled Jacobi's attention. She looked over her shoulder and almost passed out. The constant purr was coming from an idling engine—a sleek luxury car's engine that belonged to none other than Malone. He had appeared out of nowhere.

"Baby girl," Malone yelled out the driver's side window. "I just wanted to make sure everything was good with you and that you'll do what you promised to do with my number. And I really need to holla at you about some important biz. Come talk to me for a second." He held his hand up to Alek. "Hands off, Alek."

Jacobi froze. She didn't know what to do or which boy to answer. She needed to tell Alek that she really didn't have a boyfriend, but she also didn't want to make Malone wait, for fear that she'd lose her shot at being a filmmaker. He was, after all, the guy who had the connections.

"Introduce me to your brother, and I'll get you out of this mess," Yummy whispered, walking up to her with spittle and doughnut crumbs flying out of her mouth.

Jacobi turned to look at Alek but was met by the front door slamming closed, then a repetitious click of locks. Disappointment crawled through her, and she was immediately annoyed with Yummy for ruining her moment.

"So you gonna hook me up with your brother or what?" Yummy asked.

Jacobi looked at the oversized girl again. She hadn't known her brother to be prejudiced about a girl's size, but she knew he was dead set against plain sloppiness. She shook her head. "Sorry, Yummy, or whatever your name is. It ain't gonna happen. Plus"—she nodded her head toward Alissa's closed front door—"it seems my problem just cleared itself up." She walked past Yummy and headed toward Malone's car.

Yummy wheezed as she inhaled, and her nostrils flared as she stepped in front of Jacobi. "What did you say? Did you just tell me no, heffa?"

Everything was moving so fast. Malone was waiting, Yummy was challenging her, and Shooby had just sent another text asking her whereabouts and informing her that Katydid had moved, which surprised Jacobi. It wasn't like Katydid to up and move and not tell her first. Katydid's disappearance scared Jacobi, because that meant something was wrong. Excitement, fear, and worry now shot through her veins, overshadowing the disappointment she'd felt about Alek just seconds ago. She eyed Yummy, and, scared or not, she wasn't going to back down. She knew that once a bully knew they had you, they'd always start trouble. Jacobi balled her fists and stepped up. She was getting tired of silly girls, and wondered what her parents thought was so safe about this new neighborhood. In less than an hour, she had been forced to go head-to-head with verbal assaults. "I got your heffa, all right. I said—and I *didn't* stutter—it ain't gonna happen. You are not my brother's type. And if you ever bother me again, I'll make sure you never become his type." She sidestepped Yummy and moved quickly to an awaiting Malone.

Yummy bit her lip and nodded slowly. A weird smile spread across her face and she laughed. "You know what, Diggs's sister? I like you. At least I think I do. At least enough to warn you to stay away from Alek—he's mine. Plus, you're not scared of me. That has to be a first around here. I respect that," she yelled.

"Malone, is that offer of a ride to the motorcycle show still good?" Jacobi asked, almost skipping toward him.

Malone walked to the passenger side of the car and held open the door for her. "Absolutely. To and from and to get a bite to eat, too, if you want, my little filmmaker."

# 8

# KASSIDY

Her knees were numb and her calves were burning, but she refused to get up. Kassidy crawled the few feet to the side of the bed and lifted the ruffled bed skirt. There was nothing underneath except for a few dust bunnies. Unfolding her body slightly, she sat back on her heels, pressing her lips together in thought. There had to be something somewhere that she could use against her monster of a stepsister. Yummy's dresser drawers held only awful clothes; her closet, even worse outfits. And her room, in general, was a cesspool of what-not-to-wears and things that had collected so much dust and mold that they appeared to be science projects. Taking one last glance around the room, Kassidy couldn't think of anywhere else to check for dirt she could use against Yummy. Then her eyes landed on the juice-stained mattress. A spot she hadn't yet checked.

*Ahh*, she thought, then knee-walked to her cell phone

to see if Carsen had texted her back. She'd texted him almost an hour ago to see if they could reschedule, and he
hadn't responded. She was growing more panicky and
livid by the second. For some reason—probably her need
to have several male friends to make up for not having
Brent in her life—she worried that she wouldn't hear
from Carsen again, and she despised her evil stepsister
more with every tick of the clock. Yummy had crushed
her freedom and now seemed to have demagnetized her
pull on Carsen. And she couldn't have that. She needed
Carsen, his motorcycle, and as many opportunities to
learn about her new neighborhood and city as she could
get. He was supposed to be the vehicle to help her
achieve her goals. Plus, she remembered, he was cute.
That was an extra bonus.

She knee-walked her way back over to the bed, deciding she'd have to deal with getting in touch with Carsen
later. With all her might, she used her strength to lift the
yucky mattress. Unsurprised, she found crumbs galore,
and snack cake and cookie wrappers—all empty, of
course. Just about to lower the Serta, she saw a small yel-
low sticky note on the edge of the top right corner of the
box spring. She dropped the mattress, made her way to
where she'd spotted the paper, pushed her fingers under
the fitted sheet, and pulled out the note. She read it
aloud.

"Prom Choices: Alek / white boy. Six four. Fifteen. Size
twelve shoes, extralarge shirts. Single. Phone number,
five-five-five-dash-eight-two-five-three . . .' What does the
rest of this say? Her writing sucks," she said, straining
to make out the last two numbers. "Ah, got it!" she ex-

claimed, then began reading the rest. Yummy had quite a list of guys she liked and wanted, and, to Kassidy's surprise, Romero's name was on the list with two stars next to it, and there was some other guy named Diggs on there. There was a row of question marks next to his name. She wondered who he was and stuck the paper into her pocket.

Satisfied that she'd finally found something she could use against Yummy, Kassidy stood, messed up what she'd cleaned up while searching through the cesspool of a room, and walked out. If Yummy wanted to play, they would play. Overtime.

Her phone vibrated in her hand just as she was closing Yummy's door, and a smile spread across her face. Romero was calling while Yummy was walking into the house. *Game time.* Kassidy rolled her eyes at a snarling Yummy.

"Romero!" Kassidy announced his name almost at the top of her lungs, happy to hear from him. Happier that she could see panic on Yummy's face. "Thank you for last night. I had so much fun."

"Me too. What's up? Still unpacking and having family day?" he asked while chewing something.

"No. Waiting for you."

Romero laughed, and she could hear a smile in his voice. "Cool. I'm right around the corner."

Kassidy threw on her best sexy voice, like one she'd heard in movies. "Well, I need you to make either a left or a right, whichever's gonna get you here first and the fastest." She hung up the phone and casually looked over her shoulder at Yummy, who stood stuck in place with her mouth open wide enough to house a small beehive. It was Kassidy's turn to snarl, then she capped the nasty look with a huge grin. "And you, Ms. Snack Queen, I'm gonna need you to stay out of my way. Company's coming, and I think he's allergic to two-legged female dogs who like to set up people for punishment," she said, then walked toward the front door without a care in the world. As far as she was concerned, Yummy could kiss what was turned her way.

"Uh . . . young lady," her mother said, walking out of the kitchen and curling her finger in a come-here fashion. "You do know I can hear you, right? You've said nothing but bad things about Yummy starting trouble, yet you're the only one I ever hear bad-mouthing. Don't talk to her that way. Okay? You two are sisters, like it or not."

Kassidy just nodded, startled that her mom was home and glad that she hadn't caught her in Yummy's room. If she had been caught, the punishment would've been worse than one day at home. "*Step*. We're *step*sisters."

Her mother playfully thumped her head. "A hard head makes a soft behind. Well, as long as I'm your manager and you want to go on this interview that I just set up, you'll be whatever I say. Right?" She handed Kassidy a note with the details, then turned and winked, walking out of the room.

Kassidy followed her mother's wink and saw Yummy. She stood against the wall with crossed arms and a scowl across her face. "We ain't *step* nothing," she whispered, loud enough for only Kassidy to hear. "Model my foot."

Kassidy rolled her eyes. She couldn't believe that

Yummy had had the nerve to eavesdrop so blatantly. She took another look at her mother's stepdaughter and reconsidered. Yes, she could believe it.

"Whatever," Kassidy growled back. "You're just jealous."

"Do you want the interview or not?" her mother asked, returning back to the room and pointing to the note she'd given Kassidy. "Read it."

"Yes!" Kassidy said, looking at it and pumping her fist in the air. She kissed her mother on the cheek. The interview wasn't just any regular meeting. It was one with the best modeling agency in Los Angeles. One that could secure her a spot with big-name designers and major magazines. "Gotcha. No bad-mouthing," she promised. She dialed Faith before she reached the screen door, and was giving her a run-down of the details before her feet touched the porch. Her phone vibrated against her ear while she was talking, and she excused herself from her conversation with Faith while she checked to see who was calling. *Unknown Caller* floated across the screen.

"God! Why do they keep calling me?" she said, putting the phone back to her ear.

"Who's calling you?" Faith asked from the other end, panic in her voice.

"Someone keeps calling anonymously. You okay?" Kassidy asked. "You sound rattled."

Faith laughed. "Sorry. I can't help it. I kept getting strange calls, too; that's all. You know you can program your anonymous calls to go straight to voice mail," she said, then told Kassidy how to do it.

Kassidy put her phone on speaker, then did as she was instructed. "Thanks, Faith. You've been great. So are we meeting up later?"

"I'll be here in New York until next week. Hopefully, I can track down Brent by then. I've been asking around. But no luck so far," Faith told her.

"Okay, cool. Call me later so I can tell you all about my Cali boys. I got Romero, but he's just someone to talk to. No love there. Then there's Carsen—a fine piece of something who's taking me out on his motorcycle—"

"Did you say Larsen?" Faith interrupted.

Kassidy laughed. "No, silly. Carsen. Carsen with a C. He rides with this motorcycle club. He's sixteen, I think, with braids."

"Umph," Faith said. "I thought you said Larsen. Anyway, I gotta run. I'll call you later." The line disconnected.

*What was up with Brent?* floated through her mind a kazillion times in two seconds, and she could've kicked herself for never remembering his agent's name; and, like most people nowadays, he didn't have a landline at home, just a dedicated fax that was never turned off. She was angry at herself for losing contact with Brent. Then she reminded herself that it wasn't her fault. No one did home numbers anymore, she hadn't expected her boyfriend to come up missing, and it'd only been a few days since the move, so how was she supposed to think that far ahead? She was a model, not a psychic.

Romero had zoomed to the front of the house, killed the engine on his moped, hopped off, and was headed Kassidy's way before she reached the bottom step. His smile was as big as hers when he walked up to her with outstretched arms. "Gimme some love," he said, as if they were a couple.

Kassidy looked over her shoulder and saw Yummy peeking out the blinds, as she knew she would. Squaring her shoulders, she turned up the sway in her walk, sashaying her way to Romero. She'd promised her mother no bad-mouthing, but she hadn't said a thing about messing with Yummy's self-confidence. It was showtime, and if she didn't know how to do anything else, she could put on an act and make all kinds of artificial emotions register on her face as if they were real. As a model, she'd perfected the art of showing emotion, or the lack thereof, for photo shoots. Today, her look said happy, loving, wanting, and *I'm yours.* "And love you'll get. I missed you," she replied, laying it on thick and walking into his embrace. Then she shocked them all—Romero, Yummy, and herself—by giving Romero a big kiss on the lips. It was only a long peck, but it was still more than she'd planned.

For seconds she'd gotten lost in his embrace, and had momentarily forgotten that she was acting. His breath was minty and inviting from the gum he'd been chewing, she noted while her lips were pressed against his. The kiss was almost too good to pull away from, and she almost opened her lips and made it a real kiss. But she stopped herself. She couldn't fall for the first boy she met because that wouldn't leave room for her to go out and explore her other possibilities. Plus she prided herself on never getting attached or kissing someone with an open mouth, except Brent. She flirted, but didn't cheat—not completely. Lip-locking was just lip-locking, not too different from giving her grandmother a peck. Besides, to her, there was no single guy worthy of having her all to himself. None in the Cali area, anyway.

"Wow, I didn't expect that," Romero said, licking his lips and smiling.

"Me either," Kassidy mumbled, still perplexed by the feelings running through her. "Sorry," she apologized. "I didn't mean to go so hard—"

"Hard?" Romero laughed, cutting her off. "Kassidy, you can go as hard as you like with me. A little tongue would've been okay, too. I don't just go around hanging out with girls all night for nothing. You may not be able to tell, but I'm not exactly easy for a girl to get. I have standards." He laughed again.

Kassidy turned and saw heartache in Yummy's eyes, and knew without hesitation that Romero was the most important person on Yummy's list of prom choices. She didn't care how many names were on it; Romero was the one Yummy really liked.

"Excuse me?" a deep male voice asked from behind them.

"Oh my God," Yummy muttered loud enough for all to hear. She walked down the porch steps dragging her jaw on the ground.

Romero gave Yummy a strange look, and Kassidy made a mental note of it, then turned and forgot how to speak or blink or breathe or remember. In fact, every guy she'd ever seen or talked to or flirted with or wanted, including her one and only, Brent, was erased from her short-term memory. The dude in front of her was that fine.

"Hey. You all right?" the fine guy asked, pulling her from her semicomatose state. "I'm looking for an address around here. You know where twelve forty-five is? I'm looking for this older dude's house for my pops, and can't find it."

Romero walked over, nodding. "Nah, homie. She can't help you. She's new around here. But I gotcha," he said, then told the guy how to reach his destination.

"Good lookin' out," the guy said, giving Romero a pound. "I'm new around here, too. Name's Diggs."

Kassidy nodded, understanding why Yummy's jaw was to the ground. Cali was looking more promising by the day. First, Romero had given her something to do. Then Carsen had given her something to look forward to. And now Diggs, the one from Yummy's list, the dude that she hadn't even exchanged words with yet, had given her reason to forget New York, if only for the moment.

"He's cute, huh?" Yummy asked, suddenly by her side.

For once, Kassidy had to agree. "Yep, yeah, and yes. Who is he?"

Yummy laughed, then elbowed her. "Don't know. I've never seen him before," she lied.

Kassidy threw her a sideways glance. Yummy wasn't being truthful. Diggs's name was on the list of Yummy's prom choices, which Kassidy had in her pocket, and she was just about to pull it out to let her stepsister know she was aware of her lying. But then something happened. Diggs smiled and awoke something in Kassidy. Something that intrigued her far more than his being delectable. "I know him," she said, sure they'd met. She didn't know when or where, but he was too familiar. She stared at Diggs, taking in his height, muscle tone, and stance. He didn't look or stand or present himself like a regular dude. As he put one foot in front of the other, making his way down the block, she knew without a doubt exactly who he was because he didn't walk like a regular guy, either. She'd been trained as a model, and she'd bet her last breath that he was a model, too.

"Excuse me," she said, chasing after him.

"Where are you going?" Yummy asked, trying to catch up. "You're on punishment. Remember?"

Diggs turned and warmed Kassidy with a beautiful, perfectly even smile. "Are you talking to me?"

Kassidy nodded. "Yes. I know you," she said, stopping feet from him.

He shook his head. "I don't think so."

Kassidy bit her lip, wondering why he hadn't taken the bait. She'd given him the opportunity to say he'd like to get to know her better, as had almost every guy she'd ever said it to. But no-go. "I do," she tried again. "I'm not sure where I know you from, but I do."

He walked closer to her, put his hands in his pockets, and hit her with the smile again. "Is that your way of saying you'd like to know me?" He drew his eyebrows together and stared into her eyes without the least bit of interest.

Kassidy was taken aback. "Um. I'm not sure." She shook her head, more baffled than she'd ever been in her life. His asking her such a question and not flirting with her wasn't what she was expecting.

Yummy walked up, inviting herself into the conversation. "Hey!" she sang to Diggs, confectionary sugar encircling her lips.

"Go away," Kassidy hissed as low as she could.

Yummy widened her eyes, then rolled them. "That's why you're out here looking like that," she spat back in a whisper, pointing to Kassidy's feet.

*Oh, no!* Kassidy looked down to where Yummy pointed. On her feet were her ragged house shoes, which were clearly too small and holey.

Diggs looked down at her feet, then huffed what seemed to be a laugh. He looked back at her face and nodded. "Well, since you're not sure, when you find out if you are sure—and if we ever see each other again— then you can let me know." And with that, he turned and walked away.

Kassidy's pride stuck in her throat, and it took everything in her to swallow it and keep her head high. She'd never been turned down by a guy before, and found rejection hard to bear. Diggs had stood there, inches from her face, and hadn't been swayed in the least. His not being moved by her, moved her to a place she'd never before been: in the chaser's seat. She shrugged. Life was life. And one thing it'd taught her was that being in the presence of one boy could help her stop thinking about another. She hadn't heard back from Carsen, which would normally kill her ego, but that was already dead, thanks to Diggs. She couldn't find Brent. Romero was only her friend. Diggs wasn't interested. She only hoped Carsen was available as she made her way back into the house to call him.

# WHERE THE BOYS ARE

# 9

## *JACOBI*

Jacobi picked up her phone for the gazillionth time, checking for a text message or missed call from Shooby. She looked at the blank screen and cringed. Nothing. Nada. He hadn't reached out at all. In fact, she hadn't heard one word from him since the day of the motorcycle show almost a week ago, and even then he hadn't said much other than they'd have to talk later and that he'd try to find out where Katydid had moved to since Katydid's cell had been disconnected, and Jacobi couldn't call or text her. A flash-mob notice had been sent out, and he was on "duty" using a Harley-Davidson motorcycle as a stationary surfboard while holding a sign and singing "Respect," an old Aretha Franklin song, at the top of his lungs. Some of the crew danced wearing Blues Brothers–style black fedoras and sunglasses. The demonstration had been ordered by the American Federation of Flash Mobbers: A For the People and By the People Teen Citi-

zens Group to urge consumers to use less gasoline because it is damaging the ozone layer. It had been beautiful, Jacobi remembered—what she'd seen of it. She had
gotten to the show seconds before the demonstration was
over, and Shooby hadn't seemed too happy about her tar-
diness and lack of participation.

"So, what are you going to do?" Alissa asked, reading
the directions on a box of hair dye while rifling through
Jacobi's closet.

Jacobi tilted her head. She didn't know what Alissa
was talking about. The girl had come over with hair dye
that she insisted Jacobi needed to lighten her hair, availed
herself of the contents of their fridge and their candy,
then talked the whole time. But Jacobi hadn't heard her
because she'd learned how to tune her out. "Do about
what?"

"I told you, already. The set." Alissa stuck a lollipop in
her mouth.

"What set?"

Alissa laughed. "You know, set? As in party. My parents are having a family gathering, party-type thingy up
the coast, at my great-aunt's beach house by Santa Bar-
bara. They said I could bring friends along," she said.

Jacobi was about to decline when Alissa mentioned the
magic words.

"Did you hear me? They said friends—plural. Maybe
we can invite other people . . . like a cute boy or two, and
maybe you can invite your unboyfriend."

Now Jacobi perked up. Going away with Alissa's family would provide her with a great opportunity to have

Shooby all to herself. She could get away from her mother and siblings, shoot a few lives and stills, give the stock market a rest, and relax somewhere on the beach in a new swimsuit next to Shooby. *Ah*, she thought, daydreaming. *It would be fantastic.* "I could film the gathering. You know, as a gift for the invite."

Alissa almost peed her pants, or at least she looked like she was about to, jumping in place and wiggling. "That'd be hot. My mom would be so floored, she'd love us forever." She stopped hopping and sat on the bed. She deadpanned Jacobi, her eyes full of seriousness. "So, are you going to finally confess now? You were so anxious to get to the motorcycle show—I know what that means. You can't hide him forever."

Jacobi smiled. Alissa was right. If she went to the family gathering, Alissa would find out all about Shooby, so she might as well tell her. She nodded. "Okay, but he's not my boyfriend," she began.

"Yet," Alissa interrupted. "Wait until he sees your hair. I'm gonna hook you up."

"Yet," Jacobi parroted, loving the sound and possibility of it all. Then she spilled all about Shooby—their flash mobbing, and their history together, including Katydid and her part in it all. Jacobi even told her about tonight's plans for another flash mob.

"Oh, cool. I can't wait to meet your friend, Katydid. I like that name. Oh, and I heard about that flash mob thing," Alissa said, continuing to eat her lollipop while getting started on Jacobi's hair. "It was on the news—not about tonight, just about it. It seems really cool and

really fun, too, at least the proactive ones where the mobbers aren't doing illegal stuff. Can I do it, too? I can pretend to be your assistant or something. I mean, if you're
going to shoot the scenes, why not really shoot the scenes
like a professional, Jacobi? All professionals have an assistant. Go all the way—do a documentary. I mean, the
news is always broadcasting the hoodlums doing it . . ."

Jacobi had gone deaf after *documentary*. Alissa was
right; there was good being done by some flash mobbers,
stories that never made the news because they weren't
bad news. She was just the one to show the world the
good side of it. She raised her brows and her hopes. Who
knew? The Cannes Film Festival showed amateur films
all the time. Maybe she could win an award and help hu-
manity at the same time. Tonight, she'd tell Shooby
about Alissa wanting to join, then run the idea by him of
a short documentary. She was certain he'd go for it. He
was becoming more popular with each demonstration,
coming up with his own flash-mob ideas to help their
local community and their own crew. Shooby and Katydid had started their own crew as a spin-off of the federation's, and it was growing in double digits. She
closed her eyes for a second. "God, thank you for the
creativity. Now, if you can send the boobs and clear skin
just as fast . . ."

Jacobi thought she was going to die. She'd never been
so anxious in her entire life, and was sure that she'd ex-
pire from nervousness. She was standing between
Shooby's legs while he leaned against the lifeguard's
chair. The setting sun warmed her skin and, she was sure,

if she turned around she'd be able to see her reflection in his eyes. The golden highlights that Alissa had convinced her to get danced in the breeze, and her hopes rose higher. She felt beautiful, but never would've admitted it because not only had she always taken pride in being herself—a makeup-free, jeans-wearing, and comfortable-shoe kind of girl, but *pretty* required too much work. Plus it wasn't one of her strong suits. Plain was her game. Luckily, she had Alissa, who hadn't been too lazy to transform her into a girlie girl, one that they hoped Shooby would be attracted to. Knowing she was to meet Shooby, she'd abandoned her trademark gear and dolled up in a periwinkle sundress her mother had bought because she'd heard they were all the rage. Jacobi looked down and smiled. The dress clung in the right places, meaning it hid her lopsided breasts.

"You know, Jacobi, you look different today," Shooby complimented, or at least she thought he did. But she couldn't be sure he liked her look. She'd never seen him with a girlfriend, so she had nothing to compare herself to.

"Trying something new," she said, unsure of how to answer. She'd let Alissa paint her face and curl her hair, and it made her feel so good about herself inside, her feelings radiated out. Now, from her bright, new perspective, everything seemed perfect. She only hoped he liked her, too. "About the text I sent you . . ." she began, then bit her lip, thinking how to proceed and trying to keep still. "I think it'd be a good idea to document what we're doing."

"Uh-huh. Stay still," he said. "I don't want to pull your hair out."

Jacobi froze, remembering why she was standing between his legs. Something was stuck in her hair, and he was getting it out.

"Got it," he said, pulling the object out along with some of her hair. "It's a piece of candy. Looks like a piece of a lollipop."

*Alissa.* "Ow, that hurt." Jacobi turned, looking him in the eye. She stood less than a foot from him, and didn't want to move.

"So, what were you saying? You want to film me?" He laughed coolly. Flirtatiously.

Jacobi nodded. "And I want to bring someone into the crew. My new friend, Alissa. She can help me if you don't want her to be a part of the new mob. I tried to call Katydid to see if she'd mind, but she didn't answer her phone. So I guess it's up to you, right?"

Before she knew it, Shooby's lips were pressed against her forehead. She closed her eyes, giving in to the moment. He'd never before kissed her or shown the slightest interest—not like this. And though it wasn't a real bona-fide kiss like a boyfriend would give a girlfriend, she'd take whatever affection he offered. A smile stretched her lips wide, and she relaxed her neck, leaning into him, hoping he'd wrap his arms around her. But no-go. Just like that, it was over. His mouth disconnected from her face.

"I knew you were good for me. Look at you, Jacobi . . . bringing someone in. It's cool. Both ideas: filming me and a new flash mobber. As a matter of fact, I was sorta thinking the same thing, just with a different twist."

Her head tilted in curiosity.

"That's what I wanted to talk to you about. I want to do a thing sorta like they did on MTV back in the day. You know, the confession booth. I wanted to do that either before or after the flash mobs. I'm putting it together to help *our* community—*our* people. You know, *us* versus the Man?"

Jacobi just nodded. She really had no idea what man he was talking about, but she'd listen. She'd do whatever it took to get his attention, and she'd act interested as long as it meant one-on-one time for them.

"You know, Shooby. There is this other thing I wanted to ask you about, but it wouldn't involve the flash-mob crew . . . just you. Well, you and me."

He nodded. "I'm listening, baby."

"Well, I've been invited up the coast to a party. A beach-house party for grown-ups. I was thinking of filming the get-together and having some fun, too. And I've already cleared it with my parents, who won't be there, by the way. Think you'd be interested?" She crossed her arms, waiting for disappointment.

Shooby stared into her eyes and licked his lips. A faint smile spread on his face as he looked her up and down like she was the best thing he'd seen in a long time. Suddenly, his palms were on her cheeks, holding her still. "You're wonderful, Jacobi. I'm glad you're on my team. So glad," he said, then pulled her face to his and gently kissed her.

" 'Ey, Shooby-dooby-doo," one of the flash-mob crew called out, interrupting their kiss. "Ready when you are."

Jacobi's eyes stretched wide. "I thought it was only supposed to be us . . ."

Shooby looked around and laughed. "Look around. It is only us. They're calling from the other side of the hill. Guess you didn't get the text. We got a spot to hit in forty minutes. Get your camera ready. It's going to be a long night. First we mob, then me and you finish. Cool?"

# 10

# KASSIDY

K assidy clutched her résumé and portfolio and wore a smile as she pushed through the heavy door to the modeling agency. Her watch read nine forty-five, and her appointment was at ten o'clock. She nodded, happy with herself for not running behind. Her morning was going great, and the excitement of it all was cruising through her veins. She'd phoned Carsen this morning to make sure they were still on for tonight. Every night, for almost two weeks, she'd rung him—and she'd never missed one—they'd talked on the phone for hours before she turned in. She couldn't have been more ecstatic. Carsen had been just a phone call away ever since Diggs had cold-shouldered her, and he'd been more than pleased to fill the hours that normally would've belonged to Brent. She still wasn't able to get through to Brent, but she wouldn't give up hope. He was her only major link to New York, as far as boys were concerned, and she wouldn't let him go. And now, she was here at the agency. Early. After years in the business, she'd learned from latecomers that being fashionably late wasn't ever in fashion and landed models zero gigs. Being on time and being ahead of it were two of the ways she'd banked so much. Yes, her day was going great. Positive anxiousness made her heart skip beats as she checked in with a hard-smiling, blue-haired receptionist, who seemed bipolar. At first the lady was friendly, grinning bright enough to light up a night sky, but after Kassidy had given her name and the receptionist searched the calendar, the lady had become lukewarm, instantly killing her infectious smile.

Kassidy took her in. The lady seemed young. Too young to be working behind the desk. Her blue hair was cut symmetrically, with perfect Asian bangs. She wore dark gray shadow and pale lipstick. Kassidy hunched her shoulders. If it worked for the lady, then it worked for her. She wasn't the one who had to walk around looking like a cross between the Cookie Monster and the dead. Kassidy went to her seat, looking over her shoulder, not knowing what to expect. She wasn't sure if the blue-haired lady would announce to the agent that Kassidy had arrived for her appointment or throw a telephone at her. But she was certain of one thing: the woman had rolled her eyes when she thought Kassidy wasn't looking.

"Okay . . ." Kassidy said, taking her seat and wondering what had the receptionist's panties in a bunch. She'd been polite, had arrived on time, was scheduled and not making a cold call, and hadn't arrived talking on her cell phone. She rattled off all of her done-rights in her head, and, she concluded, she'd done everything correctly. If only she'd handled her personal life as well as her business one, she was sure she'd have found Brent and, possibly, would've snagged Diggs.

Other than her long nightly talks with Carsen, her days had been empty. Sure, she still had an ever-ready Romero, but he was only a friend. A cute one, but still no one she'd look at as more than a brother. She only played with him to have something to do and to make Yummy mad because Yummy wouldn't dish on Diggs.

"Kassy?" the blue-haired receptionist called, messing up Kassidy's name.

Kassidy stood. She'd correct the lady later, and put her in her place for being rude. She was, after all, a lowly receptionist who made less in a year than Kassidy had banked in a day. "Yes?"

"We're not taking any new clients." There was a smirk on the receptionist's face.

Kassidy's eyebrows shot to the ceiling. Never in her career had she encountered such a lack of professionalism, and she knew business wasn't handled this way. She was a professional with many credentials to her name, and she'd had a confirmed appointment. An appointment that had an e-mail attached; an electronic mail message proving that the agency had gone after her and not the other way around. "Excuse me?" she asked, talking herself down. She wanted to snap, go off, tell Ms. Blue-haired Bipolar that doctors prescribed mood stabilizers for her disorder. But she thought better of it. The modeling industry was small, and she didn't want her name smudged.

The lady looked at her as if she had dirt on her face. "No more new clients. Sorry."

Kassidy nodded, pressing her lips together. "Okay. Can I just leave this then? In case." She held up her portfolio and résumé package.

"Not unless you want to waste it. We're booked for this season. And a bit of advice: next time keep your appointment."

Disguising her irritation, Kassidy forced a smile on her face, then reached into her pocket and pulled out the e-mail appointment confirmation her mother had given her. She showed it to the receptionist. "According to this, I'm here on time for my appointment. The appointment that was made because your agency requested me."

Ms. Blue-haired took the paper and looked at it. She looked at her computer monitor, then shrugged. "Must be a mistake," she said, shrugging. "This says something different." She swiveled the monitor around, pointing to the screen. "See," she said, turning the screen back around before Kassidy could see it. "Next time . . ." she repeated, her expression more twisted and nasty than before.

Kassidy walked out, shaking her head. She knew without a doubt the woman was either on meds or needed some. She'd kept her appointment and was on time. "If this is supposed to be the best Los Angeles has to offer . . ." she mumbled, hoping the date she'd set up with Carsen tonight would turn out better.

Her favorite shoes were missing. Gone. Well, only one of them, she noted, searching through the closet. Zebra print pulled her attention. Kassidy knelt down, reached behind an unpacked moving box, and grabbed the right shoe to the set. She fought to free it from where it was stuck. How it got back there, she didn't know. But it wasn't right. Kassidy raised her brows, confused. She hadn't worn them since moving to Los Angeles, and was a certified neat-freak when it came down to her footgear. She kept her kicks in clear plastic containers with pictures taped to the outside, neatly stacked according to type and color. Misplaced shoes had never been a problem for her before. And today wasn't the day to start. She had a date with Carsen. A real, live, *vroom-vroom* motorcycle date with him.

"Where's the left shoe to this one?" she questioned, rattled. She had already picked out an outfit. One she was sure Carsen would love, that she'd bought months ago to match the designer shoes. "Oh well," she huffed, deciding she'd just have to switch clothing.

Sliding hangers across the bar, she diligently searched for another outfit that would be good for riding. Nothing caught her eye. She shook her head, deciding she'd have to work from the bottom up. She had to find shoes first, then match the clothes to them. She selected a clear shoe box, then pulled it out of the pile and removed the lid. One shoe was missing from the box. Now she was clearly baffled. "Ugh," she huffed, then selected another box, then another, and one more. All of her left shoes were missing except for the pair she had on: the dusty pair of too-small house shoes, complete with the hole on the bottom.

Then she had a thought. "Yummy!" she yelled, speeding out of her room. "Yummy!" she screamed continuously, storming through the house. "I'm gonna kill you!"

Her mother appeared from the kitchen, cradling the house phone and making a mean face at Kassidy. "I'm on the line," she mouthed. "With the modeling agency to see what happened. Stop yelling."

"Yummy took all my shoes, and she's not here to give them back," she said. "And I have a date. A date and no shoes."

"Just put on a pair of mine, and we'll run to the mall," her mother mouthed, her hand coving the phone. "Just please quiet down. No one's going to want to hire you if they think you spaz out."

Kassidy looked down at her mom's feet. They were three sizes smaller than hers, so the suggestion was no good. In mime fashion, she pointed to her size tens, then her mother's sevens.

Her mother pointed to the house slippers Kassidy wore. "There has to be a mistake. I'm sure Yummy wouldn't take your shoes. Gimme a sec, and I'll drive you. You're just going to have to wear those or go borrow some of Yummy's."

There was nothing in the world that could make Kassidy put her feet in anything of Yummy's. She'd die first. "I'm going to kill her," Kassidy spat. "Kill her!"

# 11

# *JACOBI*

Her head was barely off the pillow when her mother walked in unannounced and called her name. Jacobi yawned and stretched, wondering what the problem was, because there definitely was one. Her mother always knocked. Always since the move, anyway. But not today, and her fingers not rapping on the bedroom door before she entered told Jacobi something was up.

"Get up," her mother said, snatching the sheet off Jacobi.

Jacobi jumped up, anxiousness running through her veins. And fear. Had her mother learned of the flash mobbing? Or had she found out what time Jacobi had snuck in? Last night, she'd met up with the crew after receiving one of Shooby's texts, and hadn't made it home until almost ten o'clock. They'd met at one of the crew's houses, back in the garage where no adults could hear, to begin mapping out the "biggest flash-mobbing scene to ever hit Los Angeles," as Shooby had put it; but weren't able to finish because an important flash-mob alert had been posted on one of the social networks they belonged to. They'd wound up at the movie theater, where they'd all stood up, one by one, during the peak of the action in one of the country's most anticipated blockbusters and recited lines from the Declaration of Independence, while other flash mobbers did the same during a few Disney films. They'd been asked to leave and the cops had been called. Jacobi, holding her camera, had gotten it all on film, and barely made it out before arrests were made.

"Okay," her mother said, swiping her hands against each other as if dusting flour off them. She hustled to the window and opened the blinds, then about-faced and made her way to Jacobi's closet. "I just heard about the big invite from Alissa and her family. And I'm sure you don't think it's a big deal, but I do." She slid hangers back and forth, obviously looking for something. "I'm glad that you're doing other things now—making new friends, stepping up and away from the old neighborhood and the Lancaster troublemakers you were forced to be with. Katydid was nice and all, but limited . . . You have to understand, honey," she explained. With a few outfits over her arm, she sat down on the bed. "For many years your father and I couldn't afford to give you and your brothers a better life, but now we can. I want you to know that life has so much to offer you, Jacobi. But you have to accept it. Do like Diggs—he's running with his opportunity. He's already getting letters from colleges because of his test scores, and the modeling agents can't get enough of his look."

Jacobi stared at her mom, wondering what the big deal was and why she was so giddy. So she'd been invited to a party—who cared? She'd received many invitations before, so she didn't see it as huge, like her mother was making it out to be. And Diggs's modeling and getting scouted for colleges wasn't new. He'd always been smart and handsome; their moving hadn't caused that. "Okay . . . ?" she said, sitting up and looking at the outfits her mother was holding. "I'm not really understanding what the excitement is for."

"The excitement is for you, Jacobi," her dad said, leaning against her bedroom door, smiling and winking. She knew the wink was his way of thanking her for her latest stock tip. "But it's also for her. Your mother. Seems we've all been invited to the beach, and your mom's finally made some new friends that she can be proud of." He rolled his eyes when her mother's back was turned. "But I won't be going. I have a conference. Mandatory." He stressed the last word as if he was disappointed, but the exaggerated wipe of his forehead that accompanied his statement said he was glad he wouldn't be tagging along.

"That's not entirely true," her mother explained. "It's just finally nice to be around people I fit with. I mean, gel. That's the phrase you teens use, right? Gel with? Anyway, Alissa's mom asked if you could go, and then invited the rest of us when I told her I'd never been to a beach house."

Jacobi's idea of having a few days alone with Shooby died. She'd never be able to bond with him if her family was at the beach party. There'd be no way her mom would go for that. Shooby was a part of the old neighborhood, and therefore not someone her mother would want around. To her mother, everything—their old apartment, her previous school, even the way she used to dress—were all to be traded in for their new life. The life Jacobi hadn't asked for.

"So, let me get this right. I was invited, then you found a way to get invited?" Jacobi didn't see the fairness in it all. Her mother wanted Jacobi to make new friends and do new things. And now that she was giving her mom what she wanted, her mom had found a way to fit herself into the equation.

"Yes. This is going to be a *family* vacation! Now, let's get up and get to shopping. These clothes—" her mom began, outstretching her arm and shaking her head, "these won't do. I don't see why you have an aversion to dresses."

*Aversion?* Her mother was clearly taking her college classes too seriously. She'd never used words like that before.

"A virgin," Hunter said, walking into the room. "Why are we talking about virgins? What's a virgin?" he asked.

Jacobi didn't know what was wrong with her little brother, but clearly it was something. In the last few months it seemed that all his words were related to sex.

"No, honey, a-ver-shun. It means dislike." Her mom pinched his cheeks and kissed him. "Okay, Jacobi. Get dressed so we can go. You'll need sundresses, a swimsuit, halter tops. I'm forewarning you: the only clothes I'll buy are girly ones. No more tomboy stuff for you. Period. Especially now that you're starting to fill out."

Jacobi looked down at her lopsided breasts. *Fill out?* She picked up her pillow and began tugging on each end. *To the east . . . to the west . . .*

"I don't see a problem with the way she dresses," her father stated. "People push girls too hard, then complain when they wind up fast and loose," he stressed, then shook his head and walked away. "Women. I tell ya," he muttered as he made his way down the hall with her mother and five-year-old Hunter on his heels.

Sundresses and halter tops pervaded her mind while she discreetly did her chest exercises. She couldn't wear the clothes her mom wanted her to wear if she couldn't fill them out. Especially a bikini, she thought. How was she supposed to impress Shooby with mismatched breasts? "To the east. To the west. To increase your breasts. To the east. To the west. To increase your breasts!" she sang, pulling on the ends of the pillowcase, making her chest muscles expand and release. "Please, God," she began, then stopped. Her mother had said she was starting to fill out, hadn't she? Jacobi looked down at her breasts and her eyes widened. Sure enough, they looked fuller. They hadn't *grown* grown, as in a new cup size, but the smaller one was trying to catch up with the bigger one. "Thank you, God. Now, if you can just . . ." Jacobi began, whispering.

A knock on the door made her swallow the rest of her prayer. "Who are you talking to in there?" her mom asked.

"Uh, no one. I was just singing under my b[ ] cobi lied.

"Oh, okay. I just wanted to be sure. You

neighbor is a doctor. I thought I'd have to have her refer you to someone," her mother said, then laughed.

Yes, Jacobi knew what Alissa's mom did for a living, and she was no doctor. She was a nutritionist. Alissa had told her that when she questioned whether Jacobi had an eating disorder. "You wanted something else?" Jacobi asked.

"Oh. Yes. I forgot to tell you we'll be riding with Alissa and her mother to the mall. Your dad's using the car to take Hunter to a birthday party, and Diggs will be doing whatever it is that Diggs does. So that means it's just us girls. Yay! Girl shopping and girl power," her mother sang, clearly too excited for Jacobi's taste.

Jacobi struggled across the lawn, carrying a box filled with cookbooks her mother had selected for Alissa's mom. Her camera hung from her shoulder like a purse, swinging to and fro with each step, knocking against her side as she made her way to her neighbor's driveway. With every thump she grimaced, watching her prized video camera. Her mother dedicating herself to teaching Alissa's mom how to cook was fine with her, but having Jacobi carry the full load was too much. Her camera was precious, more precious than any of the recipes she was almost sure Alissa's mom hadn't asked for. If anything, Jacobi bet, Alissa's mom had probably shown some interest in a dish or two, and her mother was taking her teacher role too far. She was barely into her first semester of culinary school, and already thought she was a professor.

"Hey . . . weren't you supposed to call me?" Alek asked from the driveway.

Jacobi moved her stare off the camera and onto him. Her eyebrows lifted. "Huh?"

Alek smiled. "You were supposed to call me," he said matter-of-factly, then made his way to her.

Jacobi crinkled her nose in thought. She didn't remember telling him that. Or had she? He'd asked her to have Diggs call him, or was that Malone? She was starting to mix up the brothers. Not a good thing. "I was?"

Alek reached out and took the box from her. "Yes. That's why I gave you my number, in case you needed me. And it seems like you need me now; otherwise you wouldn't have been carrying this, Ms. Don't Gotta Boyfriend," he teased.

Jacobi laughed, moving the camera from her arm and looping the strap around her neck. "Oh, I'm sorry about that."

"Sorry that you really don't have a boyfriend, or sorry that you're one of my brother's up-and-comers?" He winked. "Be right back," he said. "My mom's been waiting for this—we've all been waiting. Cooking isn't her strong suit, and I think hers has been killing us. You should thank God for your mother. She's become a saint around our house since she started giving my mom lessons." He laughed as he jogged to the house with the box.

Jacobi followed his steps, then sat on the po[ ] did he mean by her being one of Malone'[ ] comers? She wasn't going out with Malone. Ou[ ] her eyes moved down to her chest, and disappointment crawled through her. Her breasts—well, at least one of them—had started growing, but you couldn't tell through her clothes yet. To her, they were both still too flat.

"You spill something?" Alissa asked from behind.

"If I did, it'd roll straight down," Jacobi answered. "I'm just that flat."

Alissa laughed and came out onto the porch. She sat next to Jacobi. "Oh, you mean your chest?" She stared at the semiflatness that should've been Jacobi's breasts. "They'll grow. That's not a problem. There are plenty of ways to jump-start development."

Jacobi's eyes lit. Just the thought of Alissa having a cure made the shopping trip worthwhile. "Really?"

Alissa nodded with a twisted expression. "Of course." She looked behind them. "Later though, okay? Here comes the pain in my butt."

Alek emerged, nodding his head to a beat no one heard but him. "You two ready to roll? I'm taking Dad's car."

Jacobi tilted her head. "I thought we were going shopping," she said to Alissa.

"We are. Just us three," Alek said, pulling her up by the hand. "It seems a bikini is in order—that's what my mom told Alissa. I figured, since I have such good taste, I'd help you pick one out. Unless you wanna be like every other girl and wait on Malone."

Alissa rolled her eyes. "Never mind Alek, Jacobi. It's just sibling rivalry. He wants to be Malone."

# 12

# KASSIDY

Her mother sped off, leaving her at the busy mall entrance in a state of double dustiness. Puffs of dust clouded the air where her mother's tires had spun, and Kassidy's house slippers looked like they'd been dipped in sand-colored soot. She looked down at them. No, they weren't nasty-dirty like most of Yummy's belongings, but they'd still classify as unclean if she saw someone else in them, and that was totally unacceptable.

Holding her head high, she owned her dusty slippers as if they were the best things on the planet and followed the other shoppers. She hoped that her air of superiority would make people focus on her upper region, not her feet. But her clothes wouldn't help her avoid attention, she noted, taking a good look at herself as she passed an enormous storefront window. She'd left the house as is, donning a retro Havana T-shirt and ragged-cut, high-water boyfriend sweats—an outfit she'd normally never wear outside—and had topped it off with a Panama Jack hat and oversized shades, thinking it made her look like a star who was trying to avoid the paparazzi. She'd figured if no one could see her baby-browns, no one would ever be able to prove that they'd seen her. To her, eyes were like fingerprints; they were unique and identifying, and if no one saw hers, she could pretend she didn't see them. Still, though, she had to admit, anyone would probably know it was her.

With focus and determination to quickly find the best pair of shoes to go with her outfit to go riding with Carsen, she moved through the mall. She looked at her watch as she approached the escalators, then relaxed a bit. She still had hours, and that was more than enough time to buy kicks, she thought, searching left, then right, looking for the trendy boutique she'd spotted the last time she shopped. She knew she needed to buy flats; they'd be more appropriate for motorcycle riding. But sexy, multicolored, strappy stilettos begged for her attention as she graced the store's entrance. Like a junkie, there to feed her shoe addiction, Kassidy scooped up one of the ice pick–thin heels, two three-inch ones, an all-season boot, and a wedge flip-flop. Cradling the bundle of display shoes, she held them to her chest and made it to a bench. In a second, she'd switched from her slippers and into her first choice, and with one foot inches higher than the other and her heel hanging off the back of the too-small shoe, she limped to the mirror. She spun, admiring every angle. Even though the shoes from the display didn't fit, she knew she'd found what she needed for tonight.

"Can I help you?" a blue-haired salesgirl asked, zoning in on the ill-fitting shoe Kassidy had on. Her hair was cut symmetrically with a perfect Asian bang, she had at least five shades of gray on her eyes, and her lips were paler than the law should've allowed.

Kassidy almost laughed. *The receptionist?* "Wow . . . I didn't know you moonlight at the mall. You forgot who I am already?" she asked rhetorically, knowing that the woman had to know who she was. "Yes. I need to see all of these in a size . . ." She paused, unable to finish. Stretching her neck, she looked over the racks of shoes to the men's section in the back. "Oh no . . ." Her heart palpitated and her mouth went dry. The fine guy, Diggs, was turning around toward the front of the store where she was, calling out to the salesgirl. Worse, he'd not only be able to spot Kassidy, he had a full view of the entrance, which meant she had no escape.

"What size did you say?" the receptionist-slash-salesgirl asked, still not acknowledging that she knew who Kassidy was.

Kassidy dropped to her knees, forgetting about the shoes and the blue-haired girl. She needed an escape, and the small rack in front of her would have to do until she could figure a way out of the store. There was no way she could let him see her looking like this, all ragged and homely.

Shaking her head, the girl walked away, laughing. "Let me know when you need something."

"No," Kassidy yelled in a low whisper. "Don't go . . ." But it was too late. Holding on to the display rack in front of her, she eased up a bit, trying to spot Diggs and avoid being seen. Now her heart dropped. He was headed toward the women's section, toward the space she now occupied. Frantically, she searched for a new place to hide. She looked left, then right, then made a complete circle. Her eyes turned into saucers when she looked out the display window. *Faith?* "Can't be. She's still in New York," she said to herself, watching a girl zoom by who looked so much like her friend it was scary. Then she heard Diggs's voice, and it sounded like he was only clothing racks away. To her relief, people were circulating through the area she hid in, and without thought, Kassidy grabbed the first person she saw, snatching her like she knew her, and using her for a shield.

"Hey!" the girl yelled, trying to pull away.

"Sorry. Please help me," Kassidy begged, her face pressed against the girl's back. She'd crouched as low as she could, and held on for dear life. "This guy is in here. This superfine dude who I must have. Diggs. And I can't let him see me. Not like this. If you help me get out of here without him seeing me, I'll help you. Twice. Two for one—you can't beat that."

The girl stiffened and seemed to be thinking, then laughed. "Really?"

Kassidy cringed. From the girl's reaction, she was sure she'd be on her own. "I'm Kassidy. What's your name?" she asked, hoping the girl would view her as person if she knew her name, and not as a nutcase. She needed the girl's sympathy.

"Jacobi. My name's Jacobi. And you promise to help me, right?" the girl asked, turning around and looking at Kassidy. Her eyes widened into saucers and a look of recognition covered her face. "I'll really need your help, but it may be more than twice . . ." She paused, letting her words sink in.

"Boy help?" Kassidy asked. "I can do that."

Jacobi laughed. "If you can help me with boys, why can't you help yourself?"

Kassidy snickered. The Jacobi girl was good. Really good. "Trust me. My problem is I came out of the house dressed like this. Other than that, I'm good in the boy department."

Jacobi stiffened and stepped sideways while Kassidy stepped with her. Her body language told Kassidy there was a problem. Maybe Diggs was coming their way.

"Jacobi? Is that you?" a guy asked.

"Um. Um. Yeah. Hey, Malone . . . I'm here with your sister and brother," she said, clearly nervous.

"Ah. If I had known that, I would've come home early so I could drive you. Alek's a bit new at the driving thing," he said, his voice getting louder by the second— an indication that he was walking their way, Kassidy presumed.

Jacobi looked at her watch and grunted. "Oh no. Not now."

"Keep cool, Jacobi. I can help you with him. Whoever he is," Kassidy promised. "But you have to help me out of here."

"Okay," Jacobi whispered. "But he's not really the problem. My friend's gonna be here any second, and I can't let him see *him*."

Kassidy drew her brows together, trying to figure out one *him* from another *him*, then decided it didn't matter.

*This Jacobi girl must be a player like me,* she thought, and that was more than cool with her. "Just repeat after me and you'll be good. The Malone dude will go away. Say this: 'I'll be finished over here in a second. I'm getting ready to look at some girly things . . . things that I'd like to keep private. If you know what I mean. Maybe we can meet at the food court when I'm finished,' " Kassidy instructed.

Jacobi parroted Kassidy's words, and Malone smiled.

"No problem. Alissa and my mom have broken me in with all the female stuff. I'll let you handle your girly thing," he said, his words getting fainter as he moved away from them.

"Whew," Jacobi said. "Thanks."

Kassidy laughed from her crouched position. "I told you I got you. Now, if you'll return the favor . . ."

"Diggs!" Jacobi yelled out, making Kassidy tense up and dig her fingers into Jacobi's arms. "Ouch," she said to Kassidy. "Stop!"

"What are you doing?" Kassidy questioned in a low whisper.

"I trusted you. Now trust me," Jacobi whispered back, then turned her attention. "Diggs? Can you go back to the men's section and see if they have a pair of calf-high purple Chucks in a size seven? They don't have my size up here in the women's section." She waited for a second, ignoring Kassidy's question about how she knew Diggs. "Now! Move now!" Jacobi hissed to Kassidy, almost running out of the store backward, shielding Kassidy as she shed the display shoe and picked up her slipper, then moved toward the exit.

Kassidy, with only one slipper on, grabbed Jacobi's arm and they blazed through the mall, whirring past other shoppers. They turned one corner and almost collided with someone. The same someone who looked like Faith, Kassidy thought, but couldn't be sure. Jacobi had taken the lead now, and she pulled Kassidy, hightailing it to a nearby bookstore. Like two girls on the run, they moved through the small crowd that'd gathered for an author signing and made their way to the back, between two large shelves.

Kassidy, with slipper tucked under one arm, stuck out her hand. "Again, the name's Kassidy . . . the one who owes you for real. It's nice to finally meet you. Formally." A huge smile spread on her face.

Jacobi smiled, showing off braces.

Her skin wasn't smooth, and her hair and clothes lacked style. A major overhaul, Kassidy thought, making a mental checklist of what she could help her newfound friend with, as Jacobi took her hand and shook it.

"Jacobi . . . the one you'll repay. Now, let's handle your shoe problem."

Kassidy bit into her garlic pretzel, almost ashamed at herself for enjoying the buttery carbohydrate treat so much. Usually she tried to keep her indulgences in check, especially when she had an upcoming photo shoot or runway event scheduled. But not today. After leaving the bookstore and finding Kassidy a pair of shoes and new outfit to slip into, Jacobi had insisted they stop at the Pretzel Place, located in the center of the mall, and had purchased one for each of them. Kassidy, out of hunger, lingering anxiousness, and not wanting to be rude, couldn't resist. Not that it'd add an ounce of fat to her figure. She ate carefully out of habit, because of her profession, not because she needed to. She couldn't gain a pound if she tried.

"So how long you been shooting?" she asked, pointing to the camera Jacobi wore like an oversized necklace.

Jacobi finished chewing. "With this one? Not long. But I've been dabbling with cameras for years. Just recently moved to film." She stopped talking and began looking around. "I'm here with some friends. They were supposed to meet me in the boutique to help me pick out a swimsuit for a party." She whipped out her cell and texted someone.

Kassidy's eyebrows rose at "party." It'd been so long since she'd been to one, she'd almost forgotten what one was like, and wasn't certain she wanted to be reminded. Besides—she looked at Jacobi—she was certain that Jacobi's crowd was different from her own. Kassidy was an A-lister, not B, and, missing out on fun or not, she couldn't move down the list and party with the average crowd. "A pool party? That's cool. Is whoever your *he* is—you know, the one who's meeting you here—going to be there? If so, I can help you with your swimsuit, too. I kinda know a lot about fashion, and I have some clothes in my closet that I'm sure no one at the party will have. We can dress you in something hot—and not off the rack. You'll be the It girl at the pool party."

Jacobi smiled. "Beach-house party. Up the coast," Jacobi corrected. "And yes, he's going to be there. I wish I could invite you, but I'm a guest. Me and my whole family are going."

Kassidy plastered a smile on her face. She couldn't let Jacobi know that she wouldn't go to the party if someone paid her to. She just didn't do anything that she felt was beneath her.

"There they are," Jacobi said, pointing down the corridor. "My friends . . ."

Kassidy looked to where Jacobi pointed and saw a girl taller than she, who had a blaze of red hair, and a guy who looked more like a portrait than a person. He was shockingly gorgeous and someone she'd normally go after. But she couldn't do that. Not because her boy roster was full with Romero, Carsen, and Brent, but because Diggs was walking with them. "You never said how you knew Diggs," she said.

Jacobi turned and smiled. "Diggs is my brother."

Kassidy gulped. Maybe a beach-house party wasn't such a bad idea. "Good to know . . . That means we're neighbors. So maybe I can stop by and help you with your boyfriend problems?"

# 13

## JACOBI

Jacobi leaned against the rack of basketball jerseys, scrolling through her e-mails and text messages. She'd just received a message from Diggs asking where she was, and two messages from Shooby: an e-mail about rating her sex, and a text that said he was two doors down from the sneaker store. A nervous energy ran through her body. Alissa, who knew about the flash mobbing and had signed up to participate, was there, but so were Kassidy and Alek, who knew nothing about what was getting ready to go down. She hoped Kassidy could handle it and that Alissa had found a way to get rid of Alek. He was cool, but she didn't want him in her business. More importantly, she didn't want Alek to tell Malone what she was into, and that bothered her because she shouldn't care what Malone thought. She nodded to Alissa, indicating now was the time to get her brother to leave the store, then closed out her text and highlighted her e-mail account. She opened the message Shooby had sent. The questionnaire he'd forwarded was interesting, if nothing else. And would've been too intrusive if she didn't like him. She wasn't comfortable talking about her body parts, things she'd do when alone with a guy, rating boys she'd been with, or anything like that. She was private, and hadn't even thought about most of the questions, let alone done them. She'd kissed Shooby. That was it.

"Why are you grinning?" Kassidy asked, walking up to her and reaching for her phone. "Can I see?"

"Shooby. That's why she's grinning. She loves him," Alissa answered. She said something to her brother, then turned back to Jacobi and Kassidy and kept rattling on, even after they were clearly ignoring her.

"She talks a lot," Kassidy whispered, taking the phone from Jacobi's hand. "So, he is the one, huh? Shooby? That's his name?" she asked, then began reading the e-mail. "He wants you to rate your sex . . . interesting. Didn't think of that. I need to do that like yesterday."

Jacobi smiled. This Kassidy girl seemed to really have it together, at least in the confidence department. There was no way—or reason—for Jacobi to rate her sex. "So you think I should answer the questionnaire?"

Kassidy grimaced. "Uh . . . let me see." She pressed her lips together in thought, pointing to her temple. "Hecky no. I was talking about my needing to e-mail someone. We don't do sex questionnaires or anything demeaning. Remember that." She began looking around as if she'd lost something, then turned to Jacobi. "What happened to Diggs? He was just with Alissa and her brother."

"Jacobi," Alek said, interrupting them and walking

over to her. "I'm headed to the food court to grab something to drink and a bite. Can I get you anything?" he asked, standing close.

Jacobi shook her head and a faint smile came over her face. "No, thank you." Alek was so cute and nice, but he was Alissa's brother and not Shooby. More importantly, if she had to choose between the brothers, her choice would be Malone. But he was way too good for her.

"You sure?" He swept a hair from her eye.

"I'm sure, Alek. Thanks."

He bit his bottom lip and lifted his head slightly, making himself even taller than he was. Looking down at her, he seemed to be sizing her up for something. "All right. If you change your mind . . ." He raised his cell phone in the air, then turned to Alissa and Kassidy. "Y'all be cool. Alissa, check me when you're ready, and I'll meet y'all at the car."

Kassidy's eyes bulged, and she nudged Jacobi. "Um . . . something you're not telling, Jacobi?"

Jacobi shook her head. "What?"

"Serious? You must be playing. You have to see that he's interested . . ." Her voice trailed off and she began looking around, then turned back to Jacobi. "You never said what happened to your brother. It was like he was here one second, then the next"—she snapped her fingers—"gone."

"Who knows? He may've caught up with Malone. They know each other," Jacobi began, then stopped to listen. She heard his voice before he entered the store, and her heart fluttered and butterflies swarmed in her stomach. Shooby walked in with six other members of the crew, looked her way, and nodded. A half smile was on his face, and he looked like he owned the store and his followers.

"Cobi-cobe! What it do?" he greeted Jacobi, quickly walking past her. "It's showtime, baby! Let's rock this role," he said, excited about the show they were getting ready to put on.

Jacobi grinned harder than before. He'd called her *baby* again. There was just something about him that caused her to melt. She grabbed her camera, checked to make sure it was ready to shoot, and stared at him, waiting for her cue. "I gotcha, Shooby." Then she eyed the crew again. She didn't see Katydid anywhere. "Where's Katydid?" she asked, looking at his back. He was already on his way to the front.

"I told you she moved. No one knows!" he said.

Kassidy nudged her so hard Jacobi was sure her ribs were bruised. "*That's* Shooby?" she asked, seeming somewhat surprised; and something else Jacobi couldn't pinpoint. "I dunno . . . Seems to me there's a better option lingering. The one you're not telling."

Jacobi ignored Kassidy and moved toward the checkout counter, positioning her camera. Loud music blared from a nearby oversized boom box that one of the crew had brought in. The bass was thick, banging as if real drums were attached. She couldn't help but nod her head to a Lil Wayne track as she zoomed in on Shooby. He jumped up and down in place, then began dancing in a jerky rhythm. Suddenly, as if he had springs on the bottoms of his feet, he jumped on the counter while the rest of the crew hopped onto benches in the store. They all screamed at the tops of their lungs, then gyrated their bodies. Today's flash mob was for the community, and they were making their message clear, telling the customers that hundred-dollar sneakers were sold to keep "our people" down.

"Don't buy into the lie," Shooby demanded. "The Man's shoes are meant to keep *us* down. *We* buy shoes instead of food. *We* buy hundred-thousand-dollar cars instead of homes. We invest in fashion, not education! It's time for a new nation . . . Today's revelation is get outta our situation. Don't buy the lie!" he yelled as various crew members chased customers out of the store.

Jacobi felt her body being pulled, and her zoom on Shooby shifted as she was moved closer to the exit. She snatched her arm away from whoever was pulling her. She couldn't turn to see who it was for fear she'd lose the shot of Shooby. He was in rare form, more daring than she'd ever witnessed before. There was something dangerous about the look in his eye, and as scary as it would've seemed on any other day, today it was beautiful. Sexy. "Stop!" she finally said, but it was too late. Her feet were lifted off the ground and her butt met the tiled floor with a thump and a slide. "Dang!" She'd safeguarded her camera on the way down. She couldn't let anything happen to it.

"Get up!" Kassidy yelled. "Let's go. Now!"

Jacobi was about to protest but saw Shooby and the crew running out of the store. The flash mob was over. With Kassidy's help, she stood up and made haste, following behind Kassidy, who continued to pull her. "Wasn't that great?"

They turned a corner, then another, dashed through the food court, and made it outside. Kassidy bent over, resting her hands on her thighs while she caught her breath. She shook her head. "That was awful," she said between gasps. "It was awful, base, negative. Unnecessary."

"Hey, you okay?" Alek asked, holding money in one hand and a drink in the other. "I saw you run by when I was about to pay for my food." He held up the dollars to confirm his words.

Jacobi nodded, smiling. "I'm fantastic."

"Yes, you are," a different voice answered.

Jacobi turned, and so did Alek and Kassidy; and Alissa, who'd somehow made her way out of the mall. Malone stood there, smiling.

"You said to meet you in the food court, not outside of it," he said. "I never would've guessed you'd make me *chase you* chase you."

Jacobi swallowed hard. All eyes were on her, and that made her nervous. She looked to Kassidy for help, and noticed the surprised look on Alissa's face. She knew the exchange had to be weirder for Alissa than it was for her. Alek and Malone were her brothers, and she was Jacobi's friend. Jacobi and Diggs clashed from time to time, but Jacobi had never witnessed sibling rivalry to this degree.

"Sorry . . . What did you say your name was?" Kassidy asked Malone.

"Malone," Alek answered for his brother, then side-stepped next to Jacobi and Kassidy. "His name is Malone, and he's my superstar brother." His statement was sarcastic.

"O . . . kay," Kassidy said. "This is a bit thick."

Malone's eyebrows shot up, and his words were few. "Stop it, Alek. Let this one go."

Alek ignored Malone and handed Jacobi the drink he held. She gave him an appreciative half smile. "I bought that for you, you know," he said.

Malone nodded toward the drink Jacobi held and shook his head. He looked at Alek and repeated, "I said let this one go, Alek. I'm not playing."

Jacobi looked from person to person, boy to boy. It seemed like it was only days ago that she was a nobody: a plain girl with uneven breasts, bad skin, and braces, whom no one would take a second look at or befriend in the new neighborhood. Now she had Alissa and Kassidy as friends, and options. Choices in guys. Shooby, who'd held her heart for years, had kissed her and said he'd go away to the beach house. Alek, who seemed cool as a fan, cared if she was thirsty or not. And Malone, a guy with the case of the perfects—perfectly popular, smart, and rich—was interested in her for something. She was sure it wasn't a relationship, but he was around for something.

Suddenly, like a gust of wind, Shooby breezed by, running faster than she'd ever seen him move. She raised her hand to wave and was getting ready to call his name, but he'd disappeared inside a waiting car, which pulled off before the door closed. If only she could get him to want her like Alek did, and if only he would think of her like Malone did, her world would be brighter. She had to do what she had to do, to get his attention. Maybe filling out the sex questionnaire wasn't such a bad idea, she rationalized, deciding she'd print it out and do just that when she got home. She turned and looked at Kassidy, then shrugged.

Kassidy shook her head and grunted. "Okay. I know. I know. I got you. He'll be yours."

# 14

# KASSIDY

Kassidy sat at her desk, drumming her fingers on one hand and picking up her cell with the other. She'd e-mailed Brent, attempted to send a Kassidy-would-like-to-Skype-with-you request, texted, and even dialed him again. Still, no progress. Raking her fingers through her hair, she tried to rid herself of the aggravation and disappointment that overcame her. She'd been so focused on Carsen, and now Diggs, that she hadn't concentrated enough on finding Brent to see what was wrong. Because there was definitely a problem. Had to be. She and Brent had been so close, so together, that not an hour went by without them speaking, verbally or through technology.

"Where are you?" she questioned, then looked at her desktop calendar. There was a big red circle around Friday. Faith was due back then, and Kassidy couldn't wait to hear what she had to report about her MIA boyfriend. "Yes!" she whispered, relief replacing the disappointment. She picked up her cell, anxious to hear what Faith had to say. She dialed and was sent straight to voice mail. "What's up with these phones? Faith's is never off," she said loudly.

"I don't see why you say that. *Faith* is off," Yummy said, standing by her door, chewing as usual.

Heated anger engulfed Kassidy. She opened up the Record app on her phone, set the phone down, and spun around in her desk chair. She looked at Yummy with utter disgust. "Give me back my shoes." Her words were clear and icy—loud enough to be recorded.

Yummy stood straight and stopped chewing. "Give me back my paper. I know you got it."

Kassidy got up from her seat and crossed her arms. Yes, she had Yummy's paper, but Yummy couldn't prove it. However, she could prove her shoes were gone, and that's all she needed to get the parents on her side. "I don't know what you're talking about. I didn't take anything, but you did. Why would you take all of my left shoes? What's up with only the left ones, Yummy?"

Yummy rolled her eyes. "Same reason you took my paper."

Kassidy laughed. She had her stepsister now, live and recorded on the phone. She loved her cell. She was able to record telephone and outside conversations. "I told you, I don't have whatever stupid paper you're talking about. Now give me back my shoes. I have places to be and people to meet—things you wouldn't know about."

"Oh. So you think I don't know, huh?" She bit into a candy bar. "Let me see . . . You have to meet Carsen, who, *B-T-W*, I do know," she said. "And you're supposed to meet your friend Faith on Friday. Because that's when she's *supposed* to be back from New York to give you the goods on your boyfriend, Brent, who you seem to love more than anything, which is why you keep cheating. Right?" A weird look moved over her face.

Kassidy raised her brows. How in the heck did Yummy know Carsen? More importantly, who'd told her about Brent and when Faith was coming back? "For your information, Ms. Nosier Than Thou, you don't know what you're talking about—"

"No! *You* don't know what you're talking about—for instance, Faith. Your *friend*. She's not coming back from New York Friday—"

"Yes. She. Is!" Kassidy yelled, walking toward the door.

It was Yummy's turn to laugh. "No. She's. Not." She finished off the candy bar and wiped her hands on her pants. "She can't come back from New York Friday if she's already here!"

Kassidy was just about to slam the bedroom door closed in Yummy's face, but a thought made her freeze. She had thought she'd seen Faith in the mall. Could it be that she really had?

Yummy nodded. "Let's get this straight. I don't like you any more than you like me, but our parents are married, so I gotta look out for you. If you look bad, we all do. Plus, I know what I'm talking about. Trust."

Kassidy's computer speakers rang, pulling her attention away from Yummy. Her stepsister had been right about one thing, if nothing else. They didn't like each other, so why should she trust her? she questioned as she opened the video-conference application, hoping it was

Brent. It wasn't. "Ha," she yelled to Yummy, rotating her monitor and accepting the request. Faith's pretty face appeared on the screen, and a city view that could only be a New York scene was behind her. Kassidy knew New York like the back of her own mind, and she was certain she was looking at Manhattan.

"Hey!" she greeted Faith. "One sec," she said, excusing herself to close the bedroom door on Yummy, who was shaking her head.

"Don't trust her, Kassidy . . ." Yummy's words trailed off as the door almost met her face.

"Okay, so give me the Diggs—I mean the dirt on Brent," she said, plopping down on the computer chair. "Did you see him? Did you tell him I'm looking for him?"

Faith's pretty face was serious when she shrugged her shoulders. She shook her head. "He was supposed to be at this shoot, but he wasn't. I gave one of the other models the message, though. He said Brent was working on the other side of the pond. Seems he's been there since you left. Got a last-minute shoot," she explained.

*Brent went overseas?* Kassidy pressed her lips together, pondering Faith's bit of bad news. She shrugged. It wasn't so awful. In fact, it made sense. It explained why Brent's phone was going straight to voice mail. He'd probably powered it down because international rates were disgustingly high, and he had possibly gotten a temporary overseas number until he got back to the States. It also explained why she couldn't get through to him via video conference. All she had to do now was wait for him to reply to her e-mail, and everything would be back to normal—whatever that was now. Then she could find a way to see him. "Across the pond is better than disappearing!"

Faith nodded, smiling. "Yep. I agree."

"Well, that gives me time to do what I gotta do here. I can't wait until you come back so I can fill you in on the details. There's a new one added. This guy named Diggs—" Kassidy began.

"Diggs?" Faith questioned, her expression changing. "Did you say *Diggs* as in digs in the dirt? Weird name. I thought you were seeing Carsen and someone else."

Kassidy shook her head, then caught Faith up on her guy habit.

"It certainly isn't taking you long to take Cali by storm," Faith said, a huge smile on her face.

Kassidy shrugged. "I wouldn't say that. I only went riding with Romero—who I don't like, like *that*. I only talked to Carsen, and this Diggs guy . . . let's just say he won't be easy to hook."

Faith nodded. "Well, I hate to get off, but I gotta run. We're wrapping up this series of shoots sometime in the next couple days. And you'll be happy to hear that I've notified some of my contacts and they can't wait to meet you. I told them your portfolio's current. So, we're still on for Friday."

The screen went dead before Kassidy had a chance to respond. Of course, she'd see Faith Friday. She had to catch up on the happenings in New York—the city and the industry, and her soul wouldn't rest until she did. She breathed modeling more naturally than air, and now, in

Los Angeles, she was beginning to suffocate; but that'd all change soon, thanks to Faith.

"Kassidy?" her mother's voice said, followed by a soft knock before the door opened. She popped her head inside the room. "Just wanted to tell you two things. I have to be in San Francisco first thing in the morning, so I'm flying out tonight. Right after the meeting, I'm flying to Vegas because we're going away for a long weekend, tomorrow through Sunday. Also, you have another appointment at a modeling agency tomorrow." She handed Kassidy a slip of paper with the details on it.

Kassidy's eyebrows shot up. She was confused. "I don't understand. How can I go to Vegas and be at the appointment . . ." She looked at the piece of paper with the details on it. "Thursday—that's tomorrow! Plus, I already have plans for the rest of the weekend—Faith's coming back, and she's made some appointments for me, too."

Her mother nodded. "Good. Good to hear. You needed a friend like Faith here. And we—the adults—are going on the getaway. We're still on our honeymoon!" her mother giggled. "And you and Yummy are old enough to stay home. Please don't fight. Please don't give us a reason to have to treat you two like kids." Her mother walked all the way into the room and gave Kassidy a kiss on the cheek. "Call me if you need anything."

Kassidy was ecstatic to be left alone without her mother's supervision. Her stepfather was still there, but he didn't count. All he did was go to work or lock himself in his home office. It was Wednesday night, and she could stay out as late as she wanted. Her appointment at the agency wasn't until eleven. That gave her plenty of time to rest in the morning. Looking around her room, she mentally itemized what she needed for the date with Carsen. She'd bought perfect shoes, great for any occasion, including a pair of wedge-heeled motorcycle boots, but she didn't know what else she'd need because she didn't know the complete itinerary for the day. She shrugged. There was no need to guess when she could just ask.

Her phone was in her hand and she was pressing his name in her contact list before she knew it. A dab of perspiration beaded on the back of her neck as the call connected. Why was she nervous, she wondered? She didn't do uncomfortable. She was way too confident for that. Her eyes swept over her monitor, and she knew the reason why. The picture of her and Brent that was her computer wallpaper reminded her that, like Yummy had pointed out, she was cheating.

"Ms. New York . . . the one who never takes my calls," Carsen answered.

Kassidy drew her eyebrows together, confused. She was the one who always called him, a thing she'd never have done back in New York, but here she was close to desperate for fun. She'd have to check him about it later. Now she needed to get ready, so she decided to let it go. "Mr. Cali Boy. You never told me where we're going. Girls need to prepare, ya know?"

Carsen laughed. "Indeed. I don't see why, though. You're perfect."

Kassidy smiled. Yes, she was as close to perfect now as she could get, but if he'd seen her when she had her shoe dilemma in the mall, he'd think differently. "I'll take that. But what should I bring?" she asked, and began pulling clothes out of her closet, deciding between pieces and outfits as he told her of their plans and where she should meet him.

Romero was outside in the driveway waiting on his moped when she walked out of the house. His innocent smile dug into her conscience, making her feel terrible. He was so cute, and she hated to play with his feelings. He was, hands down, a sweetie who deserved better than to have his heart and hopes toyed with, but she didn't know how to tell him that he just wasn't *it* for her. He was too available, not her idea of interesting, and seemed to have limited aspirations, like Yummy. He wanted a motorcycle like Yummy looked forward to the next treat—two things Kassidy felt were inconsequential. Kassidy shook her head. She just didn't do small-scale ambition and didn't believe in limitations; just as she didn't believe in people popping up unannounced and unexpected—like Romero had just done.

"Hi, Romero," she said, stepping off the porch and onto the sidewalk. Her bag with the motorcycle boots she'd need for her date with Carsen was over her shoulder. She was casual dressy, so there was no need for extra clothes. They were going motorcycle riding, then to an after party. Though she didn't want to hurt Romero's feelings, she had to remind herself that he had come over uninvited, so any ill feelings would be his fault.

Romero got off his moped, dug his hands into his jeans pockets, then headed her way. His smile was infectious, and though she was slightly irritated for his popping up, she couldn't help but cheese like she'd won something.

"What's good, Kassidy?" he asked, his voice trailing off. "Hey, Yummy, what's crackalackin'?"

Kassidy looked behind her and, sure enough, Yummy was there. She rolled her eyes. Yummy, with all the weight of her body and attitude, had a way of sneaking up that Kassidy couldn't understand. She'd never known such a big girl to move so quietly, especially not one who was a loudmouth troublemaker who could literally be heard breathing. She moaned under her breath.

Yummy gave her the side eye. "I heard we'll be home together all weekend. Yippee!" she said snidely. "Well, hurry along, Kassidy," she rushed, shooing Kassidy like a fly. "You don't want to be late for your date!"

Romero stopped and his smile faded. "You have a date?"

Kassidy exhaled, giving Yummy a death stare. She turned to Romero. "Just going out with some friends, that's all. There are a lot of us," she added, not wanting to hurt him. "What are you doing here?" she asked, hoping to change the subject.

Yummy giggled. It was low, and probably not heard by Romero, but it rang crystal clear in Kassidy's ears.

"Um . . . um . . . Yummy just called and asked me to stop by so I could show her some things about motor-cycles."

Kassidy's eyebrows raised and her head tilted. There were two problems with what Romero said. One, Yummy had undoubtedly set her up so Romero could see she was going out with someone else. Two, he couldn't show her things about motorcycles if he didn't have one. "Oh, really? How are you going to do that?" Her tone was dry, and it matched her attitude. No, she didn't like Romero as much as he liked her, but his doing something behind her back had peeved her.

Yummy flounced her heft past Kassidy, then beelined her way to Romero's moped. She grabbed his extra helmet and began putting it on. "He's taking me to see some," was all her mouth said, but her body told a different story. Her eyes said, "So there!" and her clothes said she had tried to dress up for him.

"Cool. Y'all be easy," Kassidy said, then gave them her back. She didn't have time for Romero or for Yummy's childish foolishness; she had bigger and more important things to do. Plus, she rationalized, Romero's thinking he'd ticked her off was the excuse she needed to make an exit to avoid further discussion about her date. Hurting people just wasn't on her to-do list. She could be nasty, catty even, but, unlike Yummy, she wasn't a bully or troublemaker. She was an accidental heartbreaker, and it wasn't her fault.

She whipped out her phone to text Carsen that she was just around the corner from where he was picking her up. She'd decided on the meeting place because she didn't give out her address. You couldn't be a real live player if all your pawns knew where you lived. She'd tried that once and found herself face-to-face with two boys at her front door. She'd vowed to never let it happen again.

"You going far?" a male voice asked over the loud rattle of a car that could've used a tune-up.

Kassidy pressed the Send button on her cell, then rolled her eyes out of habit. She just didn't get these Cali boys and the way they were always trying to lay down game when her back was turned. "Uh . . . let me see? No!" she began, then turned and swallowed her words. Diggs leaned through the open driver's side window, cruising on the wrong side of the road, commanding all her attention and making her heart drop. She didn't know what to do. The guy she wanted—a candidate who seemed unsure about wanting her—was in front of her, but the one she wanted to hang out with—a more than probable replacement boyfriend with a nice ride (if Brent didn't resurface)—was waiting around the corner. "Sorry, I didn't know it was you."

Diggs gave her a half smile. He continued driving on the wrong side of the road, which made it easier for them to converse as she walked. "It's cool. I was taught not to talk to strangers, too . . . in kindergarten." He chuckled a little.

Kassidy joined him in laughter, glad that he was showing a lighter side to himself. She was happy that he was talking to her at all, really. "Cute. Very cute. And what else did you learn in kindergarten?" She stopped, pointed her phone at him, and acted as if she were scolding him.

Diggs pulled over and put the car in park. He got out, stepped onto the curb, leaned against the driver's door, and crossed his arms. "I'm not holding you up, am I?" he asked, his tone more serious—more interested.

Kassidy cringed inside and smiled on the outside. She

didn't want to make Carsen wait, but she couldn't miss her opportunity with Diggs. There was something about him that captivated her, and she needed to figure out what it was. Yes, he was cute. That went without saying. He was also a bit mysterious, and she was certain she knew him from somewhere. But where? She tilted her head and looked at him so hard she was sure he thought she was trying to see through him.

"How do I know you?" she had to ask, tired of wondering who he was and why he wasn't swayed by her beauty like every other guy she'd met. He grinned confidently, and she was sure that not even a speck of dust marred his confidence.

"You don't, and that bothers you," he told her, reading her mind. He was cocky, and she liked it.

Kassidy stepped up, pointing her phone at him again. "I've seen you somewhere before. Somewhere other than here. I know I have."

Diggs shrugged. "Maybe. But seeing me isn't knowing me. Those are two different things."

She nodded. He was cute and quick. "But I'd like to know you." There, she'd said it, and now she felt a little better. Just a bit.

Diggs straightened, then reached out and took her phone. "That's possible . . ." He started programming something into her phone—his phone number, she assumed—and handed it back to her when he was finished. ". . . If you don't have a boyfriend."

Kassidy grew giddy inside. There on the screen was his contact information. She smiled. A high-pitched horn blew and killed her high. Without having to turn around, she could tell it belonged to a motorcycle. By the questioning look on Diggs's face, she knew it had to be a guy, and he wasn't someone Diggs knew. And if it was a dude, it had to be Carsen. She shrugged. Who else on a motorcycle would have a reason to honk at her?

"There you are, Kassidy. I was waiting for you. Ready?" Carsen asked, braking in the middle of the street.

Kassidy looked from Diggs to Carsen, Carsen to Diggs. She smiled. It was the only thing she could do.

"Well, I better let you go," Diggs said, making his way to the car and getting in.

Kassidy gave him an apologetic look. "It's not what you think. Wait a second. I'll be right back," she said quietly. She needed to work her magic, and if Carsen heard her, her show would be over before it even began.

Diggs just nodded his head. He didn't say a word, but he watched her closely.

"Hey, I didn't think you'd come!" she yelled to Carsen, making her way over to the motorcycle. She winked and puckered her lips, then blew a *shush* at him and mouthed "boyfriend."

Carsen, being the player that he was, nodded. "What you want me to do?" he asked.

Kassidy raised her brows to the heavens, glad that Carsen was as game as he'd said he was when they met. He'd said he wasn't a hater, and had now proved he wasn't. She held the sides of her phone, her fingers positioned over the screen. "Give me the address for the party. I'll meet you there in one point five," she said.

Carsen nodded. "Meet me at this address in two. One

point five's too soon for the party," he said, then rattled off some numbers and a street.

Kassidy entered the address at lightning speed, winked at Carsen as he was pulling off, and made her way back to Diggs. "Sorry about that. I had to handle something with him real quick. Now, where were we?" She bent over, leaning on the car.

Diggs laughed and stuck his head out the window. "I forgot to tell you something else about kindergarten."

She tilted her head. "What?"

"I failed kindergarten," he said matter-of-factly.

Kassidy laughed. "You failed kindergarten?" She shook her head. "Serious? Why?"

Diggs raised his brows. "I never learned how to share. Still don't and won't. Call me when you get through playing." He revved his engine and pulled off.

# 15

## JACOBI

Jacobi got off the bus and looked around, pressed for time. She only had four hours until her curfew, and breaking it wasn't an option. Her mother had told her to be home by eight, and not a minute later. They had company coming for dinner, and Jacobi had to be there. She'd made that clear. She'd also made it clear that a punishment was impending if Jacobi broke the rules. But Jacobi hadn't been to her old neighborhood in a while, and needed to absorb everything before she went to Shooby's for their meeting—and to give him the Rate Your Sex questionnaire she'd printed and filled out. Her eyes scanned the area. The broken-down cars next to the curb, which were held up by bricks instead of tires, were eyesores. The loiterers, young and old, took up residence on the block as if street corners, sides of buildings, and house porches were their homes. Jacobi was amazed at how things that never before struck her as different had become so. Before, all of the hood happenings were normal, expected. Now that she'd moved to a clean, quiet neighborhood where most all of the residents were productive, her old stomping ground was unappealing. Like a woman three times her age, she shook her head in disagreement with it all. Why didn't most of her old neighbors work or seem to want to? Why did the guys hang on the corners as if they could better themselves by doing so? She shrugged. She didn't have the answers.

Crossing the street, she made her way to the neighborhood store, owned by a Korean family. Ever since she'd moved, she'd been longing for things she couldn't find in the new neighborhood: stuff like butter crunch and chocolate chip cookies sold in the brown-and-white three-pack, flavored quarter water, and Kool-Aid pickles. All the goodies called to her as soon as she entered. She took a left and picked up the cookies, turned right to get the water, then headed to the counter to select the biggest pickle she could get. She smiled. Here, she knew where everything was and could've walked through the store blindfolded to pick what she wanted. She'd made her way up and down the few aisles too many times to count, and it made her miss where she'd come from.

"Looka here! Uphill girl done made it back downhill to swarm with the lowlifes," a familiar voice said.

Jacobi took her Kool-Aid pickle from Mr. Hyo, one of the owners of the store, and turned. A huge smile spread across her face. Her bestest friend in the whole world. "Katydid? Oh my God!" She hugged her friend and they rocked side to side. "Where've you been? I've been looking for you."

Katydid squeezed Jacobi. "I've been right here in the hood, where I'm always going to be. Where else am I gonna go?" she questioned, letting Jacobi go.

Jacobi drew her eyebrows together. She'd tried to reach Katydid a few times. She'd called her right after they'd moved to give Katydid her new home and cell phone numbers, left her a message, but never got a return call. Then she'd called again and again, and it was the same story. Finally, after hearing the automated message about the number she'd reached being no longer in service, she'd waited for what seemed like weeks, then dialed Katydid's cell again, hoping it was back on. But it wasn't. She'd even asked Shooby about her. She was certain he'd told her that Katydid had left the neighborhood, and had assumed something bad had happened or that Katydid had gone to live with her grandmother, who lived in a better neighborhood in a great school district. A good education was something Katydid wanted more than anything. Her plan included a college scholarship. "I heard you moved."

A weird expression registered on Katydid's face. "Well, as you can see, you heard wrong. I'm not leaving Lancaster."

Jacobi cringed inside. Katydid didn't sound like her old, positive, I'm-going-to-make-it-out-of-the-hood-no-matter-what self. Instead of ruining their moment, she decided to let it go. She was still stuck on why Shooby would lie to her, especially about Katydid. They'd all been so cool once, and he knew how she felt about her best friend. "Okay, it is what it is," she said, lacing her arm through Katydid's and walking out of the store.

"So you never said why you're down here slumming it with all us common people," Katydid said. "Because it can't be because of me—you didn't even know I was still here. Gotta be Shooby."

They crossed the street and walked toward Jacobi's old place. "Of course. You know that. I'm always around for Shooby," she said, laughing. "No—okay, yes. But this time I'm here for the meeting . . . you know, the *meeting*?" Jacobi emphasized, reminding Katydid about the flash-mob meeting she was sure Katydid was going to attend. Katydid was one of the founding members of the flash-mob crew, and was always so psyched about their mission—to have fun and make a difference—that Jacobi was sure she was going to be at the meeting, too. Because she didn't want Katydid to be disappointed in her, she didn't mention the Rate Your Sex questionnaire.

Katydid stopped and drew her eyebrows together. "Oh." She paused. "I'm not going. I have to meet my mom somewhere," she said, then gave Jacobi a hug. "I'll call you, okay? The bus should be here any second, and I can't miss it." She patted Jacobi on the back, then speed-walked away.

Disappointment moved through Jacobi as she watched her friend make haste to get to the bus stop across the street. She assumed Katydid's appointment must be important for her to flee so quickly. "Katydid!" Jacobi yelled, trying to stop her. "Katydid! Come back!" she called out again, but Katydid didn't stop. Jacobi grimaced. In the midst of her happiness about seeing her friend, Jacobi had forgotten to get Katydid's new number. Katydid turned sideways as if she were turning around to come back, and a glimmer of hope lightened Jacobi's heart, only to be replaced by disappointment and sympathy. Her jaw dropped. There, in the middle of Katydid's body, was a rounded hump. *A baby bump?* "No way..." Jacobi said, gathering herself and her store-bought treats. In seconds, she'd crossed the street, running to the bus stop.

"Katydid!" she yelled, catching up to her bestest friend in the whole world. Her good friend who was fifteen, like her. Her pretend sister who was also going into the tenth grade and was supposed to be a virgin, like her. She caught her by the arm. "Katydid! Really? Pregnant?"

Katydid's eyes answered Jacobi's question as the bus pulled up. "I'm so sorry, Jacobi," she said, then pulled away from her friend and boarded the bus without ever turning around.

Jacobi sat on the sofa in Shooby's hideaway, thinking about Katydid and snacking on butter crunch cookies. She knew there was a reason Shooby had lied to her about Katydid moving. He must not have wanted her worrying about her best friend, and probably didn't want Katydid to be a bad influence, she told herself. She and Katydid had been so positive once, especially Katydid. She'd been so set on going to college and making it. She'd always talked of getting out of the hood, making a career for herself, and owning a big house. "That was then," Jacobi said, wondering how Katydid could do something so stupid when she knew Katydid was so smart. Then she thought about how hypocritical and judgmental she was being. She was almost no better than Katydid, she reminded herself, remembering the questionnaire. She shook her head, deciding not to give Shooby the paper.

"I'll be in there in a second. You cool?" Shooby asked from outside the door.

Jacobi straightened up and inspected herself. She'd made sure she didn't half step on her outfit, making sure to dress as cute as possible to get Shooby's attention. She looked down at her chest, wishing it had blossomed more. "I'm good," she answered, grabbing the camera strap and pulling it taut. She gripped it with both hands and mentally recited the boob mantra: *To the east, to the west, to increase your breasts. To the east, to the west . . .* She pulled tighter each time, flexing her chest muscles as much as possible, and watching them expand and contract with each tug. By now, she was sure, she had to have the strongest chest around. If only the rest of her maturity would catch up, she'd be happier. It seemed everyone was bypassing her. Alissa had had her rite of passage, and with Katydid being preggo, her physical maturity wasn't in question. She shook her head. Kassidy, with her long legs and perfect body, was probably the definition of womanhood and had had her cycle months ago, she assumed. "Dear God, why me?" she questioned aloud.

"Why you, what?" Shooby asked, surprising her.

Jacobi jumped, shaking her head. "Nothing, just questioning . . . questioning . . ." She searched for a lie, but couldn't come up with one. She looked in her lap, twiddling her thumbs.

"Questioning what?" Shooby asked, sitting next to her, taking her attention from her thumbs. He moved close enough for their thighs to touch. "What's wrong?"

Jacobi warmed. She was embarrassed and ashamed. She couldn't tell him that her breasts weren't big enough or that Mother Nature was calling everyone but her. She couldn't make her mouth form the words she wanted to say to him. How was she supposed to say *I like you and I want you to like me*? "Nothing," she lied.

Unconvinced, Shooby grabbed her hand and kissed it. "You can tell me, Jacobi. I'm here for you. You know that, right? I'm here . . ."

Heat traveled from where his lips met her hand to her heart. She swallowed the lump that formed in her throat and begged her palms to stop sweating. She nodded. "I know." She'd become the nervous wreck that she'd seen girls become in movies, and she didn't know what to do.

"Can I kiss you?" he asked.

Jacobi almost nodded again, but then something struck her. "I saw Katydid on my way over here," she said.

Shooby let go of her hand and stiffened. "Oh God. What lie did she tell this time? She's turned into a habitual liar. What did she say now?"

Jacobi reared back her head. "Why didn't you tell me that she is . . . ya know?"

"Pregnant and stupid and don't know who her baby daddy is?" Shooby asked. "Stay away from her, Jacobi. I know that's your girl, but she's become a trip since you moved. A straight sack-chasing trip."

Jacobi's eyes widened. Shooby calling Katydid a sack chaser threw her. She'd never known Katydid to chase guys for money, and couldn't believe her friend had turned into a gold digger. "Don't say that . . ."

Shooby nodded. "Now back to me and you, Jacobi. What's up with us?"

*Us* hit Jacobi like a Mack truck. "I didn't think you liked me like I like you." The words were out of her mouth before she could stop them, and she prayed for death. If she died she wouldn't have to suffer the embarrassment of the rejection she was sure was coming, but then she thought about it. If Shooby didn't like her, he wouldn't have wanted to kiss her. A door slammed somewhere in the house, and Jacobi relaxed a little.

Shooby rolled his eyes in a masculine way, and she could see disappointment on his face. "Dang," he whispered, looking at his watch. "She wasn't supposed to be home for hours," he said, then got up. "Let's go. I don't want my moms to think we were . . . ya know?"

Jacobi looked at him sideways. "Stop playing. You know I don't get down like that."

Shooby shrugged. "Yeah. But you know how parents are . . ." He looked at his watch. "About six-thirty . . . Yeah. We gotta run. I'm—I mean we. You, me, and the crew are doing this huge thing, and I need you to film it. And we gotta figure out how you can flip us some money on the market. I know you agreed to do a documentary, but the flash mob really needs to make money to fund our operation. Maybe you can do both?"

She didn't know what to do. Her mom said she had to be home by eight. If it was already six-thirty, she had to go. The bus ride alone was going to take almost forever, and if she waited five minutes longer, she'd be late—and on punishment. Being confined to the house wasn't an option. She couldn't film her documentary if she was home. She pressed her lips together in thought, and shook her head.

"Please . . . for me?" Shooby said, then reached out, pulled her face to his, and gently pressed his lips on hers. "How can you say no to your man?" he asked, making her forget her mother, the dinner party, and her upcoming punishment.

Jacobi's lungs almost burst as she crept back into the house holding her breath. She'd somehow slipped past everyone gathered in the family room and made it to her bedroom. She set her camera on her dresser, her purse on a chair, and threw herself onto the bed. She had to invent the excuse of all excuses to talk her way out of being late. But what could she say? she wondered as a soft knock rapped on her door.

"Open up. It's me—Alissa. I saw you . . ."

Jacobi rolled off the bed and quickly walked to the door. "Did anyone else?" she asked as soon as she saw Alissa's smile.

Alissa shook her head. "I don't think so, but I can't be sure." She handed Jacobi a package. "I saw Kassidy, and she asked me to give this to you since she doesn't know where you live. She said it's some stuff for our trip."

Jacobi took the package and opened it. Inside there were all kinds of beachwear, mostly bikinis, and what looked like panties. "Oh. She doesn't?"

Alissa laughed. "I guess not. And no, those aren't what

they look like. Those are different bikini bottoms. She said no one's matching their swimsuits anymore. Seems matching is out." She shrugged.

Another knock on the door made Jacobi freeze. The only other person who'd knock would be the one who'd threatened her with punishment. Her mother. Then the door burst open, and Jacobi relaxed a little. Diggs stood there, and he was upset. "How could you be late for Dad's surprise party?" he questioned.

Jacobi's eyes bulged. "Dad's? What do you mean, Dad's? I didn't know . . ."

"Whatever. You were just out being fast. Anyway, Mom wants you downstairs. Now!" Diggs snapped, more upset than she'd ever seen him. He eyed the swimwear on the bed.

"Okay." Jacobi tried to cover up the little pieces of cloth, but it was too late.

Diggs snatched them. "What are these? What are you doing with thongs and G-strings, Jacobi? Don't tell me my little sister is turning into—"

"They're not mine." She snatched the couple pairs of bikini bottoms he held and stuffed them back into the bag. She wanted to punch him in the face, kick him in the neck, anything to momentarily shut him and his protective-big-brother-on-a-rampage mouth up.

"See you in the family room," he snarled as she reluctantly followed him, Alissa on her heels. "And if I find out you and some boy . . ." He didn't finish his threat, but she got the message.

As soon as she walked into the family room, she

smelled something in the air—trouble and punishment. Her mother's expression told it all. Someone was going to feel her wrath as soon as company left.

"Jacobi, sit down. There's something we need to tell you."

Just then, Hunter ran in holding a paper airplane. "Mom, what does *S-E-X* spell?"

Her mother almost fell out of her chair, and Jacobi had to cover her mouth to prevent herself from laughing.

"Hunter, where did you learn that? At school? Were the kids spelling that word at preschool? Did you tell your teacher?" Her mom rattled off the questions, clearly worried that someone was tormenting her little monster.

"No, it's right here. It was in Jacobi's stuff." He handed her his airplane.

Her mother unfolded the airplane and read the paper. "Jacobi!" she hissed, getting up and snatching her by the arm. She pulled her into the kitchen. "What's the meaning of this . . . ?" She held out the paper. "Are you having sex, or do you just plan on doing it?"

# 16

## KASSIDY

Diggs had gotten under her skin and raised her antennas. Now all she could think about was where he was, if he'd ever talk to her again, and what she could do to positively win his attention. Kassidy exhaled. She hadn't even captivated him yet, and already he was exhausting. He was also exhilarating, she reminded herself, and that was something she wasn't used to. Not even Brent had made her mental wheels spin like Diggs. Diggs not only whirled through her mind and made her reconsider her too-many-boys problem, which she'd never really seen as a problem before; he'd also upped his worth by refusing to share. No one had ever come straight out and made that clear. She'd never encountered anyone else like him; she didn't share, either. A guy was all hers or nothing to her. She, on the other hand, could see whomever she wanted. Carsen, Romero, and countless New York guys served as proof of her doing whatever whenever. As long as they could have moments of her time, they never complained.

A smile parted her lips. "Diggs is different, but even the different can get got," she assured herself as she turned a corner and trekked up the block, looking for something to occupy her time until it was time for her date. Glancing at her watch, she saw that she had plenty of time. Diggs's driving away and killing their conversation gave her more minutes to spare than she'd have liked. If she'd known he was going to go on without her, she could've just left with Carsen. "Nah," she said, that would've killed her chance with Diggs, she was sure. He'd made it clear that if she was taken—or appeared to be—he was off-limits.

A horn tooted, interrupting her thoughts. Kassidy looked to the street and saw Romero whizzing by. Yummy was on the back of the moped, sticking out her tongue and giving Kassidy the finger. Knowing Yummy thought she had one-upped her because she was with Romero, Kassidy waved and laughed at her stepsister. Then she halted in her tracks, and a new plan formed in her skull. The car Diggs had been driving was parked in a driveway across the street. It must be Diggs's and Jacobi's house, she thought. She didn't realize they lived so close. She knew they were all in the Hills, but never would've assumed they lived almost on top of one another. Without pause, she made her way to the house and up the short sidewalk. Her finger was pressing the doorbell before she knew it.

"Kassidy," Jacobi greeted, opening the door. "What's up?" She stepped onto the porch.

Kassidy grinned. "Nothing. I was just on my way to a party, and realized this is your house. Wanna come with?"

Jacobi nodded yes, but said, "I can't go anywhere. This lady who lives here—the lady I thought was my mother, but couldn't possibly be because of her coldheartedness, put me on punishment. Can you believe it?" she asked sarcastically, rolling her eyes.

"Oh no. So you can't have company, either?" Kassidy asked, hoping to be invited in. She had to see Diggs.

Jacobi shrugged. "Maybe tomorrow. Tonight's not a good night. Tossing a glance over her shoulder, she explained, "They're having a celebration dinner for my dad."

"Jacobi, Mom wants you." It was Diggs's voice from inside the house.

Jacobi rolled her eyes. "He's getting on my nerves. I don't know what's up with his attitude," she whispered, more to herself than to Kassidy.

"Jacobi!" Diggs's voice grew closer. "Didn't you hear . . ." his words trailed off when he made it to the door.

"Diggs," Kassidy greeted.

Diggs gave a nasty chuckle, then shook his head as if he wasn't surprised by her presence.

Jacobi looked from Diggs to Kassidy, then Kassidy to Diggs. "O . . . kay. I see I'm in the way. Check me tomorrow, Kassidy. I should be able to come out then," she said, disappearing into the house, calling out to her mother.

Kassidy leaned against the black iron porch rail, her eyes on Diggs. "So are you still caught up in your feelings? Or have you gotten over whatever trip you were on?"

Diggs stepped out of the house, stuck his hands in his jeans pockets, and looked her up and down. The tension was thick and obvious—much too intense for two people who weren't even a couple. "What's up with you? You just go around dropping by people's cribs without calling first?"

Kassidy's eyes turned into saucers. She'd never considered that she'd done the exact same thing Romero had done to her. She wasn't one to drop by unannounced, or at least she didn't used to be. This dude was definitely changing her routine. "Well, let's be clear. I was here to visit your sister—not you. We have business that doesn't concern you—that started way before you and I met. So, *no* is the answer to your question. I didn't drop by here to see you without calling first, because I didn't come here to see you. Clear?"

Diggs walked down the few porch steps, laughing. He turned and locked eyes with Kassidy. "You think you're something, huh? You got these little boys in your pocket, eating out of your pretty model hand, and now your ego's inflated."

Kassidy reared back. "How did you know I was a model? You saw my work?" she had to ask, curious.

Diggs shook his head. "Did I see your work? Huh," he whispered, parroting her words. "*You* are a piece of work, Kassidy. You know that?"

Kassidy walked up to him. She looked up, glaring. "What's wrong with you? Why are you so flip? We just met. You saw some guy pull up on a motorcycle, who you don't even know, by the way. And you assume he's my boyfriend or one of my boyfriends or whatever, and you're wrong. You act like we're a couple and I'm cheating on you or something . . ."

Diggs waved her away. "Get outta here. It's not me you're cheating on. And it's definitely not going to be me you're cheating with. I'm flip because I know you. I know your style. You're a pretty girl, I'll give you that. But pretty ain't enough, baby. Not for me. Go play with your Carsen, that little dude on the moped, and your dude in New York. What's his name?" He eyed her. "Oh yeah. Brent or something like that."

Kassidy's head almost fell off. How in the world did he know so much of her business? She hadn't told Jacobi or Alissa about Brent or the other guys. *Yummy? Has to be.* She didn't know how Yummy had gotten to Diggs already, but obviously she had. "For real, Cali boy, you need to check yourself and your sources. You clearly don't know me," she said, then walked away. She was going to make herself feel better by doing exactly what he was accusing her of: playing. And if Carsen was game—which he was—so was she. She'd rather play hard than stand in Diggs's presence and get played.

*Forget Diggs and his self-righteous, egocentric, too-good-to-share, selfish behind*, she thought, still infuriated as she got off the bus. Looking at the address Carsen had given her, she saw she was only a few houses from where they were meeting. During the whole horrid pothole-banging bus ride over, Diggs had bounced through her mind. His knowing all her business had caught her off guard, and she hoped it hadn't registered on her face. She usually had time to get into the act, but not today. She'd get him back, she promised herself. She'd make him regret making her feel less-than and low-down. It was true she'd been a player, but that didn't apply when she and Diggs met. At the time, she'd thought Brent was missing, so, in her defense, she wouldn't have been classified as a player then, she rationalized. Still, though, she felt the need to prove him wrong and knock him off of his I'm-too-good-for-games pedestal. His insistence on not sharing told her he was the jealous type, and she knew exactly how to destroy his ego. She'd reel him in, then drop him faster than when he'd driven off and left her standing on the curb like yesterday's trash.

"Where am I?" Kassidy questioned. Her thoughts were so full of Diggs, she'd forgotten to keep up with the house numbers. She stopped, reread the information Carsen had given her, then realized she was steps away from her destination, standing in front of a group of salivating guys. She rolled her eyes. Normally, she'd relish the attention, but after her confrontation with Diggs the Magnificent, she only wanted peace. Peace and Carsen, and not the disturbing feeling coursing through her veins.

"Hey, you lookin' for something, baby? Because if you are, I got what you need," one of them said.

"How could she possibly want you, when I'm right here? You want someone who's not going to talk about it, but be about it. Right, lil momma?" asked another one, rubbing his hand over his goatee and eyeing her like he owned her, which added to her discomfort.

"Leave her alone. She's with me," said a deep voice she

was certain she'd never heard before. It was strong, and obviously commanded respect and attention, because none of the guys replied. That caught Kassidy's interest.

"Thanks," she began, then turned and looked into Carsen's eyes. He was still, hands down, one of the finest guys she'd ever seen. He was cuter than Brent in a rough-around-the-edges way, but couldn't touch Diggs. He'd made it into the top three, and that was good.

"No. Thank you," he complimented, smiling as he walked up and took her hand in his. He wasn't as tall as she'd thought he was, but he had a certain confidence that made him appear taller. "Are you okay? You look a little . . . disturbed, if you don't mind me saying so. Please tell me I didn't miss too much. I'd just stepped out the house when I heard them fools tryna get at you."

Kassidy reared back her head. How Carsen had sensed her feelings, she didn't know, but it sure felt good. Carsen had erased the disappointment Diggs had caused, and she was immediately at ease with him. At that moment, she believed it was okay to tell him any- and everything, but she'd didn't. She knew better. Good moments passed, she told herself, and so did information. Your personal business could pass from one person to another like hers had passed from Yummy's mouth to Diggs's ears. "I was feeling a little disturbed and disappointed, but I'm fine now that you're here, Carsen." She flirted, letting his name dance off her tongue while he still held her hand.

"Good. Good. That's what's up. As long as I'm around, you don't gotta worry about people bothering you. Dudes like them," he said, nodding his head toward the boys who'd crassly tried to hit on her. "And just so you don't think I hang with dudes like that, I don't know those guys—they're kids." He winked. "So, can I drive you somewhere, Ms. New York? You shouldn't be walking with stray animals like that hanging around. What direction you going in?" he asked, teasing.

Kassidy laughed. She liked his game and how he kept her smiling. Flirting shamelessly, she giggled and tucked her hair behind her ear with her free hand. She shrugged and gripped his palm tighter with the other. "Well . . ." She swung the hand that he held back and forth. "I was coming to meet this really fine dude who drives a motorcycle, but now I don't know. It depends . . ."

"On?"

"Where you're going," she whispered two inches away from his ear. "Because wherever you go, I go. I'm with you."

He laughed and led her to a convertible, not a motorcycle. She almost choked when she saw it. Not that she didn't know boys with cars; she knew plenty. But in New York, where she came from, an average young guy with a motorcycle and ride like his wasn't something she saw every day. "You sure? So you trust me like that?"

Kassidy couldn't remember the last time she'd been so relaxed around such a fine boy other than Brent. As much as she'd tried to fake the funk with Diggs, she hadn't been totally at ease, not like she was with Carsen. Diggs was intimidating; Carsen was easy. He'd made her comfortable from the giddyup, and he seemed to be as carefree as she was. Plus, he came with a bonus point, one that Diggs didn't possess: Carsen was nonjudgmental.

His laid-back quality kicked in as soon as they sped off, with the top down, headed toward the main street.

She closed her eyes and basked in the warm California sunshine. Her hair did the cha-cha in the breeze, and she ignored the traffic and all distractions. She felt at peace knowing that she was sitting next to someone protective who wanted to have fun, not tie her down. A guy who'd made it plain and clear that he didn't care if she had a boyfriend or not.

"You ready, Ms. New York?" Carsen asked, pulling over to the curb.

She suppressed a smile. She'd shown him her teeth too many times in a short period, and she'd didn't want to appear eager. She was Kassidy, New York model, after all. "Ready for what?" She sat up just as a valet was opening her door.

"J's. It's supposed to be *the* spot here in LA. I thought we'd try it together."

She'd heard someone mention a J Restaurant & Lounge before, but couldn't remember who. They'd said the place was great, but Carsen had only said J's, and she couldn't see the signage from where she was. Too many people were gathered in front of the place. "You mean J's Restaurant & Lounge?"

"Yes. Aren't you hungry?" Carsen asked.

Kassidy raised her brows in thought. As a model, she didn't always eat much, and sometimes had to remind herself to do so. Other than salads, low-carb meals, and an occasional treat, she wasn't that into food. Today, though, was different. She'd sit down to a meal if it meant being in good company and not going back to her house. She didn't feel like arguing with Yummy, pretending so she wouldn't hurt Romero's feelings, or running into Diggs. She'd had enough of the foolishness.

As soon as they walked to the restaurant's entrance, her heart fell to her stomach and her knees felt weak. She shook her head. Just when she thought she could relax, she looked through the large window and caught sight of none other than the person she wanted to avoid most. Diggs. He was walking away from the hostess's stand, and he wasn't alone. She couldn't see who was with him. "God," she whispered in a long exhale, caught off guard. She leaned against the wall for support.

"You okay?" Carsen asked, curiosity on his face.

She nodded and decided to be honest. She told him about what had happened earlier between Diggs and her.

"That's all?" He snickered, wrapping his arm around her. "This should be interesting."

They entered J's Restaurant and the whole place was abuzz. They walked downstairs to the dining area, which had a lounge to the right. The waiters zipped by with pleasant smiles, and the seated patrons ate and bobbed their heads to the music that blared from the speakers. Couples danced on the outside patio and dance floor.

"Talk about deception. Who'd have known all this was behind the wall? A restaurant that plays hip-hop?" Carsen took her by the elbow as they followed the hostess toward the back. "Where's the dude at? You see him?"

She discreetly searched for Diggs and his date as they walked through the restaurant toward the outside patio. She didn't see them anywhere on the bottom floor. "Maybe they're gone."

"Maybe not," he whispered and nudged her. He tilted his head right.

She looked in the direction he indicated. Sure enough, Diggs was staring at them.

"That's them," she said between clenched teeth. "Oh God, the hostess is seating us by them."

"Good. Are you up for this, Ms. New York?" Carsen kissed her hand. " 'Cause I don't think you really know how us Cali dudes do it. Some of us don't play."

"Yes! I'm up for anything—with you." She flirted more than necessary, hoping it wasn't overkill.

After he pulled out her chair for her, he swept her hair to the side and pecked his soft lips against her neck. He put his mouth to her ear and whispered, "Throw back your head and laugh, as if I just said the funniest, sexiest thing that you've ever heard. Quick, he's watching."

She did as she was told and grabbed Carsen's hand. She held it, even as he walked to his side of the table and sat down. He eyed her curiously and bit his lower lip.

"How far are you willing to take this game?"

"As far as you are," she answered honestly, enjoying every second.

"Okay. I'll wink every time I see him looking. I'm facing them, so that gives us the advantage."

The waiter came over and his nametag read Ambrogio.

"Italian?" Carsen asked him, then ordered the food after Ambrogio nodded. To her surprise, he spoke fluent Italian, and both Kassidy and the waiter looked impressed.

"You speak Italian?" she questioned, then felt foolish. Of course he did; she'd just heard him.

"Looks are deceiving. I know it's hard to tell now," he said, running his hands over his ultraneat braids. "But I was a military brat. When I was a kid, we moved around a lot because of my pops, and I picked up a language or two. Gotta do that when you go to elementary school, if you wanna pass." He laughed. "Give me your hand. If we're going to put on a show, let's put on a good one."

Carsen took her hand in one of his and kissed it twice, as if once wasn't enough. He pulled her up from her seat. With his other hand, he rubbed her shoulder and then rested it on her lower back just above her waist. They walked slowly to the area of the balcony where couples danced.

A fast-paced remix was playing and Kassidy began to dance in step with the other partying people. Carsen stood inches in front of her, winking and licking his lips. He was too cool to get his groove on, but she could tell he enjoyed watching her. She looked over her shoulder, and, sure enough, Diggs was eyeing her, too. When she turned her attention back to Carsen, he surprised her. He cupped her face gently, kissed her forehead, then her nose, and then her cheek.

"Come on, Ms. New York." He pulled her closer, removed her purse from her hands, and held her tightly. They rocked slowly.

"Carsen, the song's fast."

"What song? I don't hear a song. I thought we were making our own music."

Kassidy pressed her head against his chest and closed her eyes. She no longer cared about Diggs and whoever he was with. That's the lie she told herself. They could have each other. She was right where she wanted to be.

"You ready?" Carsen asked. He stopped dancing.

Kassidy nodded.

He ran his fingers through her hair and kissed her softly on the forehead. "Let's go eat. I see the waiter bringing our food." He held her hand and guided her through the tables. All of a sudden, Carsen stopped short and she almost gasped aloud. She knew where they were going before they got there. She could smell the scent of competition a mile away. The next thing she knew, they were standing by Diggs's table.

"Diggs, right?" Carsen extended his hand. "I didn't get a chance to meet you earlier."

"Yeah," Diggs replied dryly, ignoring Carsen's proffered hand. The girl he was with wore a huge hat and kept ping-ponging her face back and forth, looking from Diggs to Carsen, then back to Diggs. Kassidy couldn't see past the oversized hat. She wanted to see her face, see what kind of girls Diggs liked, but couldn't. Then the girl finally turned toward Kassidy.

*Oh my God*, Kassidy thought, looking at the girl's blue hair, overly made-up eyes, and pale lips. She was the rude receptionist/wannabe model from the agency who'd chastised Kassidy for being late. The one who'd seemed to get so much joy from turning Kassidy away. She was also the salesgirl who'd sold Kassidy shoes. Kassidy held her head high, made the girl look up at her, and sneered. The girl may've been where Kassidy wanted to be—with Diggs, but Kassidy had the upper hand because all eyes—

the girl's, Diggs's and Carsen's—were on her. She may have gotten turned away at the agency, but she'd rise because that was what she did. She didn't bend. Didn't cave. She kept reaching for the top until she made it. Of that Kassidy was sure.

"Hey, thanks, man." Carsen patted Diggs on the back.

"For what?" Diggs asked, holding up his head like he was superior, which sickened Kassidy. He reminded her too much of herself.

"For messing up. Don't you know if you treat a girl bad, she'll go to the one who'll treat her good?" Carsen said, then put his arm around Kassidy's shoulder and led her away. "It's time for us to party. When do I have to have you home?"

Kassidy raised her brows. As far as she knew, her mom was already gone to San Francisco, and tomorrow her mother would be meeting Kassidy's stepdad in Las Vegas. Kassidy was free until Sunday, and could do whatever she wanted. "You don't."

# 17

# JACOBI

Jacobi was convinced her mother didn't have a heart and had adopted her as a baby. There was no way that her mom had ever truly been in love or had wanted the affection of someone else. If she had, she must've been a woman scorned before meeting Jacobi's father. Jilted. Someone must've hurt her mom badly, and her mother must've vowed to take her grief out on the real lovers of the world, like Jacobi. Her mother would make sure that she had company in the land of the miserable. Because of her mother's heartlessness, Jacobi would die of shame, and her poor father would leave the world as a lonely man whose feelings were unrequited.

*That lady*, the one who kept insisting that she'd birthed Jacobi and pretended to be her mother, wouldn't leave her alone. She was banging on her bedroom door, trying to kill her joy. Her knocking was as persistent as a jackhammer. As much as her mom tried to convince her, Jacobi knew she wasn't really her mother. She couldn't possibly be. If she were, she'd have understood her daughter, or at least would have tried to.

"Here," *that lady* yelled, jiggling the doorknob, unable to turn it. "Ja-co-bi! Un . . . lock . . . this . . . door . . . now!" she was demanding, spitting out each syllable of Jacobi's name. They'd gone through it the whole afternoon, and not once had her mother been able to open the door. One would think that she'd have caught on, but she hadn't.

*And they think teenagers are stupid.* Jacobi wasn't going to open the door, and her mother knew it.

"Fine. Have it your way, and I'll have it mine." She slid a yellowed piece of paper under Jacobi's door.

Her birth certificate.

Jacobi picked it up. *"Dang."* *That lady* was, without a doubt, her biological mother. Jacobi groaned loud enough for her mom to hear, knowing it'd tick her off.

"I told you, I'm your mother. And, believe me, right now I almost regret it as much as you do. Now unlock this door."

"I can't. It's stuck," Jacobi lied.

"And you'll be stuck when your father comes home and I show him this questionnaire like I should've done the other night. But, unlike you, his dinner party was important to me—it's not every day someone gets a promotion as big as his."

Jacobi jumped up and unlocked the door. She had to. Her father was her only friend in the house now that Diggs and Hunter had sided with her mom, and she didn't want to disappoint him. If he knew about the sex questionnaire or her plans to meet Shooby, he'd be devastated. Jacobi was his little angel who made money on the stock market for him, and made his heart feel pure with her innocence. She couldn't allow her father to believe that she'd lost her morals or values. She'd inherited her principles and drive from him.

*That lady* thrust the Rate Your Sex questionnaire in her face. "Take it."

"It's not mine," Jacobi lied again as she looked down at the e-mail Shooby had sent her. She wondered how, out of all the other things she had in her purse, Hunter had chosen the questionnaire. "Mom, I said it's not mine. Why don't you believe me?"

"I can't believe a nice girl like you would participate in such a thing. That's why I wanted us to move from the old neighborhood. Plenty of girls your age are knocked up over there. You need to go to church or something."

"Church? You don't even go to church. And what does that have to do with anything? Especially something that's not mine," she questioned, but knew her mother had a point. Katydid was preggo, and she was sure almost half of the other girls she knew were either in the same condition or would be soon.

"And you're sticking to your story, huh?" her mother said, crossing her arms.

Jacobi nodded.

"Okay . . . well, that's that, then. No beach-house party for you."

"What do you mean? We're all going. You're going because I was invited," Jacobi said, more scared now than before. She had to go to the beach house. Shooby was meeting her there.

"No, just me, Diggs, and Hunter are going. Your father can't go because of the new promotion. So, it looks like just you and he will stay here."

"But, Mom . . . I'm supposed to go film the party for them, remember? That was my gift for being invited. Do you understand what you're doing to my dreams and potential career? You're killing them—my reputation. Now everyone's going to think I'm some sort of irresponsible person who doesn't deliver. That's not how Dad raised me."

Her mother raised her brows. "I know you're your daddy's girl and all, but let's get this straight: that's how *we* raised you. And I'm *saving* you," her mother added, scowling. "Don't you see that? And, according to this other e-mail, Alissa isn't the only one you're supposed to be with at the beach."

*What other e-mail?* Jacobi wondered. "Yes, she is. What are you talking about? I didn't get another e-mail."

"I know you didn't because I did. I got it for you, then erased it," her mother said, admitting to checking Jacobi's e-mails.

Jacobi was hotter than fish grease as she watched from her bedroom window as her mother and Diggs loaded the car. As far as she was concerned, they couldn't leave fast enough. She'd been stuck in the house with them for a whole week, and all they talked about was the beach.

They'd become the *W* people. They planned *who* they would visit on their way up the coast. *What* they would do. *When* they would eat. *Why* they'd shop at one store before the others. And *where* they'd meet when they were done.

Living with them had become more like staying in a house full of crickets who mocked her with every chirp. She knew she wasn't allowed to go, so why did they keep reminding her? Hunter she could understand, because he couldn't help it; he was just a kid. But *that lady* had no excuse other than torture. Jacobi sucked it up, as her dad would say, and wiped her tears. She'd find another way to see Shooby. Even if she had the opportunity to go with them now, she wouldn't. She wouldn't want Shooby to know that she was related to insects whose ears were on their knees, because they were certainly crickets—bugs bugging her.

What had taken her months and two neighborhoods to build, her mother had destroyed in less than a day. Jacobi had promised Shooby, given him her word that they'd be together at the beach and wrap the documentary. Now her mother's heartless cruelty would make her seem like a liar—or like she was scared—or, even worse, like she'd didn't like him.

When her dad barged into her room, she jumped and accidentally dropped the blinds.

"Do you know where those things are? You know . . . those things that you girls need once a month?" His hands were shaking.

Jacobi laughed. She knew what he wanted to say but

couldn't. She loved him but couldn't help but torment him. She needed to smile, anything to get not being able to be with Shooby off her mind. "What things?"

His eyes darted. "Come on, Jacobi . . . you know . . ."

"Ohhhh," she sang. "You mean feminine products, like Tampax, Kotex, Always." She watched him grow queasy and wipe his forehead with the back of his hand. He was perspiring and shifting his feet. He had menstrual phobia and was uncomfortable with anything having to do with feminine products. He couldn't watch the stupid commercials, and hadn't even been able to be present in the delivery room when she and her brothers were born. "Try the bathroom."

"I did."

"Yours?" she asked, wondering why her mother wouldn't keep her feminine products in their master bathroom.

"No, you and your brothers'."

Jacobi lifted her brows to him. "Yours. Try yours. Look under the sink."

He shook his head. "Can't you get the stuff for her?"

"Dad, you know I'm not speaking to them."

"Please. You know I can't do it . . . my hands go limp when I touch the stuff."

Jacobi had her chance and she was going to take full advantage. "Okay, but it's going to cost you. You're pulling me away from the stocks, and there are some companies that I'm keeping an eye on . . . ones that aren't dropping as fast as the others," she said, nodding toward the ticker tape scrolling across the television screen.

"And I need to get my *Wall Street Journal* from Alissa's, too."

He nodded and sighed. "Okay. Whatever you want—anything. I'll keep your mother busy while you sneak next door, and I'll watch the Dow until you get back. Just tell me what I'm looking for."

"So, what're you gonna do?" Alissa asked, packing her suitcase as Jacobi leaned against the dresser.

"I don't know, but I'll come up with something. My dad is in my pocket. I made a killing for him on the market before, so getting him to let me go see Shooby shouldn't be too hard. I can just pretend I'm going to see Katydid."

"Good idea. So you already told Shooby your situation?"

"Haven't spoken to him . . . been trying to contact him. I hope he hasn't left yet," Jacobi said. She had to get to the old neighborhood to find him, to tell him about the change in plans. She was sure he'd tried to call or e-mail or text, but her mother had taken her phone and computer away. She hoped he didn't think she was avoiding him. It had only been days, but it felt like forever. She felt defeated.

"You sure your mom won't change her mind?" Alissa asked, a look of hope on her face.

Jacobi crossed her arms and rolled her eyes. "Impossible multiplied by two."

Alissa sat on the overfilled suitcase, trying to close it. "What about a film or investment class? The ones you were thinking about when we first met? I think your mother mentioned it to my mother, too." Alissa winked, reaching down and trying to stuff a bag of maxi pads inside and out of the way of the zipper. "Education is more important than a trip to the beach."

Jacobi stuffed the maxi pads all the way inside, then zipped Alissa's suitcase while she sat on it. She snapped her fingers. She had it. Jacobi knew what to do to get away, and felt bad for her poor father. She breathed a sigh of relief. She finally understood what enlightenment meant.

"You know, Alissa, you've got a point. My mother never said that I had to stay here with Dad, she just said I couldn't go with them." She jumped up and hugged Alissa. "If I can pull this off right, I may just meet you at the beach . . . You'll have to find a way to hide me, though."

"That's easy. The house is huge, with separate wings like a mansion. It also has a pool house."

# 18

## KASSIDY

"Oh . . ." she whispered as soon as she opened her eyes. Kassidy was stuck on stupid. She had no idea where she was. There was no computer in the corner of the room. No frilly, girly covers. No teenage voices wafting from across the street and floating in through the open window. No signs of the room belonging to her. She looked down at her clothes and saw that they'd disappeared, too. She was wearing a robe—an oversized muumuu that looked like it belonged to someone's grandmother. Her eyes kept darting. First inside the robe, where her underclothes were, thankfully, still in place, then around the room once again. She saw she wasn't in a bedroom at all. It was more like a den. A small pool table was on one side, and a huge plasma TV on the other. CDs, stacked almost to the ceiling, flanked both sides of a high-tech stereo. She rolled onto her back on the couch to gather what little composure she had left and breathed deeply. She was almost calm—that is, until she looked above her and immediately sat up. There was a painting of three almost nude hoochie mamas, doing only God knew what, attached to the ceiling. *Ohhh.* She rubbed her pounding temples.

She was in desperate need of an aspirin. Her head and her body seemed to be competing to win the title of her most painful moment. At the rate her headache was increasing, it would leave her other aches in a trail of dust.

Despite her pain, she walked around the room touching things. Normally, she wouldn't have gone through someone else's stuff. Invading privacy was more than disrespectful to her; it was degrading. But she had no choice. Whatever she could find out could help her figure out where she was and what might happen next. There was no way she was going to leave the room not knowing what she could be walking into. She fingered the objects with a white-glove touch, as though she were inspecting for dust, but the space was squeaky clean. She went back to the couch where she'd slept, and paused. She scrunched up her nose, preparing for the worst. Picking up the covers with two fingers, she took a short whiff of them. They were clean—very clean—and smelled better than her mother's laundry on good days; and her mom could wash the heck out of clothes.

"Where am I?" she whispered, and lightly tapped her foot. She wanted to yell, rant, have a fit, but she was too ashamed. She should know where she'd slept and how she'd gotten there. Kassidy had never put herself in this position before, and it bothered her to the nth degree. What kind of person didn't know where they'd laid their head? She continued her search, but there was no indication of to whom the room belonged. There was nothing personal enough for her to make an assumption. No this-is-my-lair-and-my-stuff. Nothing.

A knock on the door almost caused her to jump out of her skin. She ran to the mirror and checked herself. She might be God-only-knew where, but she wasn't going to be caught with a thing out of place; not if she could help it.

"Yeah?" she called out to whoever was on the other side of the door. "Come in," she invited, like it was her space.

A lady, around her mother's age, walked in. While there was something familiar about her, Kassidy couldn't place her. The lady grinned like she had no problem with Kassidy being there, so Kassidy smiled, too.

"It's nice to see that you're up and at 'em, sugar. Are you okay?" the lady asked, grabbing Kassidy's hand between hers. Her expression was one of concern.

"I guess. I've just got a huge headache." She played the game with her. If the lady knew who she was, Kassidy was going to pretend to know her as well. It made no sense to make a bad situation worse.

"There's some acetaminophen in the medicine cabinet. Those are better for the lining of your stomach than aspirin. Not so harsh, you know? I've also laid out some towels for you, toothbrush, face moisturizer . . . everything I think a young lady needs."

*Who is this crazy woman?* Kassidy nodded.

"Go get cleaned up and meet me in the kitchen, sugar I cooked a little something."

"Thank you." Kassidy cheesed, quite sure that she was showing more gums than teeth. "I'll be right in," she said, hoping that the lady would leave before she did because Kassidy had no idea where the bathroom was located.

After showering and applying the makeup that she carried in her purse, she went through all the toiletries the woman had set out. The spread was unbelievable, and everything was brand-new. Either the lady was out of her mind or had been expecting her—or another girl. *Maybe she has a daughter.* There were three tubes of lipstick, two mascaras (one waterproof), facial cleansers and moisturizers, and several different kinds of perfume. She hadn't missed a thing, Kassidy thought, until she held up the clothes and the underwear. They were boys' clothes and boxers. She inspected them closely, and they seemed as though they'd fit. *Well, at least they're new.* She slipped into them as easily as she'd put on her shoes.

"Sorry about the clothes. I forgot to pick up some panties and girls' clothes when I went out," the lady said when Kassidy walked into the kitchen.

"No problem. Thanks for all the toiletries. I left them in the bathroom," Kassidy said as an afterthought. She didn't want the lady to think that she'd taken the stuff, just in case the lady hadn't bought it all strictly for Kassidy's use.

"No problem, sugar." She looked at Kassidy with her head tilted. "You don't mind me calling you sugar, do you, sugar? I call everyone that." She slid a plate in front of Kassidy.

"I don't mind at all." She stared at the plate piled to

capacity with enough food to feed a small neighborhood or Yummy. She bit her lip as she stared at the bacon, wondering what kind it was.

The lady must've read Kassidy's mind. "Turkey bacon. Everything on the plate is fat free. A girl has to watch her figure, you know? But it still tastes good. Eat up—as much as you want, sugar. I'm the only one who has to worry about gaining weight around here."

Kassidy glanced at her plate, and her stomach turned. While the lady had prepared herself two egg whites, one piece of bacon, and a grapefruit, she'd made Kassidy at least a half dozen eggs, the rest of the pack of bacon, fried potatoes, toast, and pancakes. *What happened to fat free?* Kassidy was afraid to tell the lady that she also had to watch her figure. Having been a model since she was a kid, she'd been on a lifetime mission to keep her figure flawless.

Then Kassidy scarfed down her food without giving it another thought. It wasn't salad or fresh-squeezed OJ, but it was good. She figured the faster she ate, the more she'd be able to get down. It never occurred to her to worry that this strange woman might poison her. Kassidy also didn't think about asking the woman who she was or where she was. She felt an obligation to be extra nice and accommodating because of the lady's hospitality.

"Oh, sugar, would you like another helping?"

Kassidy dabbed her mouth with a napkin. "No, thank you. The food was excellent. Can I ask you something?" she inquired, unable to handle the not knowing any longer.

"Sure, sugar. What is it?"

Kassidy looked around nervously. "Where am I?"

The lady threw her head back and laughed. "I'm sorry. It never occurred to me that you might've forgotten. I guess that you don't know who I am, either. A long night will make anyone forget. I'm Lucy."

Again, Kassidy froze. What did "a long night" mean? She searched her brain for answers. She hadn't been drinking. She refrained from alcohol. She didn't do drugs—ever. She now wondered if someone had slipped her something. Had someone drugged her? Maybe she'd been given a roofie, the date-rape drug she'd heard about for years.

"Don't look so scared, sugar." Lucy lovingly patted her hand. "Nothing bad happened to you. You were sick, that's all. I mean really, really sick. Food poisoning, if you ask me. The way you were hugging the toilet . . . I had to put you in one of my robes. You ruined your pretty little outfit with all that vomiting. I'm telling you, when Carsen carried you into the house . . ."

"Carsen!" That's whose room she was in, but it didn't seem like a bedroom because there was no bed in it, just an oversized sofa. His name rolled off her tongue, and relief coursed through her like a flash flood. How could she forget being with him? she wondered. Then she remembered tidbits of the night before. The awful stomach pain that gripped her from the inside and seemed to reach all parts of her body. The projectile vomiting. Being hot, then cold, then hotter than she'd ever been before. And dizziness. She couldn't forget the wooziness and weakness.

"Where's Carsen now?" Kassidy asked.

Lucy shrugged her shoulders. "Who knows? He

dropped you off, put you on the sofa, then did like always. Kept it moving. That's what my son does."

Kassidy nodded. She guessed she should be disappointed that Carsen would abandon her when she was sick, but she wasn't. She was just glad that he hadn't taken advantage of her, because he could've. At least he cared enough to bring her to his mother. *Or did he?* she questioned. Maybe he'd brought her to Lucy because he didn't know where she lived. *That'll teach you,* she tsk-tsked herself. Being dropped off and abandoned was what she'd gotten for going out with someone she barely knew. She had to be more careful.

All of a sudden, Kassidy felt as if she were about to burst. The food was rising in her gut, begging to come out. "Excuse me, Lucy." She ran through the house and into the bathroom. Before the door was closed, she lifted the toilet seat and sank to her knees. She gagged, but nothing came out except a retching sound. Heaving, she gripped the commode, and in a matter of seconds her stomach was empty. Feeling weak, she managed to pick herself up from the floor and make her way to the vanity. She looked in the mirror; her eyes were watery and kind of bloodshot. Kassidy rifled through the medicine cabinet looking for the toothpaste. She brushed her teeth and washed her face and used the eyedrops she'd found while looking for something to freshen her mouth. She smoothed her borrowed outfit and walked out—right into Lucy.

"Sugar, are you okay? Still sick?"

"I'm okay," Kassidy said, even though she wasn't sure . . . "just a little too full."

Lucy laughed. "Well, I can believe it. You cleaned your

plate. If you want to stick around, I'll be making lunch soon."

*Lunchtime!* Kassidy panicked. She checked her watch. It was ten in the morning. She had only one hour to get to the modeling agency appointment. Her eyes scanned her clothes, and her head shook in disappointment. She'd just have to go, looking like a boy, and pray that her face and credentials could help her snag a shoot.

The door to the agency was as heavy as the last one, Kassidy thought as she pulled on it with all her might. It was as if the weight of it were a symbol of how hard it would be to get in and get signed on as one of the models. The clock on the wall told her that she'd barely made it. It was just two minutes to eleven, and her heart raced. She hated to be late.

"Kassidy Maddox. Here to see Ms. Rosschild," she said to the receptionist, who, thankfully, greeted her with a warm smile and a nod. A silent *whew* moved through her as she went to sit in the small waiting room and saw there was only one other person there. It was a guy, but his face was hidden behind a magazine. He had long legs, wore faded jeans and simple sneakers. Just from the midsection down, she could tell he was a pro. His outfit gave him away. Newbies were the ones who dressed up, and they were also the ones who rocked everyday sneakers— the ones that were trendy. Seasoned models wore the best designers, and their clothes seemed plain, but the clothing tags attested to their quality.

Her shoulders relaxed as she got comfortable in her seat and noticed the receptionist looking at her outfit.

The receptionist's eyebrows were raised, and her head was tilted as she inspected Kassidy. Kassidy gave herself a once-over, hoping that somehow she'd pulled off the boys' clothes and high heels. Still watching the clock, she saw the agent was running two minutes late, but she didn't care. She was here, and that was all that mattered. The guy with the magazine sat across from her and to the left, noisily flipping the pages. Kassidy almost rolled her eyes, but stopped herself. She didn't want to show how little tolerance she had, at least not here, so she focused on the photos on the walls. There were good shots of high-profile models, top photographers and designers, and major companies plastered all over the place, telltale signs of the talent the agency represented. Her hopes rose until the guy's magazine lowered, taking her mood with it.

*Couldn't be.* She exhaled audibly.

"Serious?" Diggs said, with a look of disgust or disdain on his face.

"What are you doing here?" Kassidy whispered across the small space.

Diggs purposely dropped his chin in a *Duh, what do you* think *I'm doing here?* expression. He tsk-tsked her, pointing to her clothes. "Long night?" His question was sarcastic.

Kassidy narrowed her eyes, then plastered on a fake smile. "Wouldn't you like to know?"

He shook his head. "Not interested . . . I'm not into doorknobs," he said, accusing her of being so loose that any boy could have his turn with her.

Kassidy couldn't help herself. She had to dig into him, and she couldn't scream or throw anything at him—not if she wanted the agency to represent her—so she did the next best thing. She got up and went over to sit next to him. "Let me tell you something, Diggs," she spat, as low as she could. "For your information, no one had a turn with me. I got food poisoning last night—at least that's what I think I got—and I had to stay with Carsen's mom. He wasn't there. I chucked all over my clothes, so I had to wear what she gave me," she explained, not knowing why she felt the need to do so. Diggs wasn't anybody to her.

Diggs surprised her by laughing. "So you had the linguini cioppino, too? I think there was something wrong with the clams. That's what you get for slumming it— and I'm not talking about the restaurant. You're lucky that food poisoning is all you got, dealing with that Carsen character. You could've wound up in jail."

Kassidy's eyes widened. "How do you know so much about me? Boys, and now what I eat? And what do you mean by jail?"

"Diggs! I'm so glad you could make it. I've been trying to get my hands on you for a while. Glad you've come to your senses! Come on back," a very petite lady said, beckoning from the entrance to the back offices. She stopped, glancing down at a pile of papers she had in her hand. "And I guess you must be my eleven o'clock, Kassidy?" she said, looking at Kassidy. "You might as well come on back with Diggs. Seems you two know one another . . . which might be good. Ralph needs a male and female. I'm Ms. Rosschild," she said to Kassidy.

Diggs and Kassidy stood at the same time.

"Wow . . . someone must've leaked it to you, Kassidy.

They're looking for an androgynous look for the girl, and your men's garb fits."

Kassidy smiled and followed behind Diggs as they followed Ms. Rosschild. "You still haven't told me how you know all my business." She purposely stepped on his heel.

"The girl I was with, you know, the chick with the blue hair—the receptionist slash wannabe model slash agent-in-the-making who was sent out to woo me for the other agency—ordered the linguini and got sick, too. Everything else I know is confidential. Let's just say you talk too much, obviously." He stopped and looked her in the eyes. "Let's just pretend we like each other, so we can get through this, and I can get up the coast."

"Who says we have to pretend?" Kassidy asked, winking.

# 19

# JACOBI

It had taken Jacobi almost two days to come up with a bulletproof plan to get to the beach house. She knew she had to be careful, because if there was just one hole in it, her dad would see through it. His foresight was eerie; he always seemed to figure things out before they occurred. His years in the military before she and her brothers were born had given him the ability to weigh every situation and proceed with caution. Under normal circumstances, she wouldn't have thought of manipulating and deceiving him. But getting to Shooby wasn't normal; it was urgent. He said he'd be able to spend one day and night with her, and she wanted every hour she could get. As much as she hated tricking her dad, she had no choice. Her time was running out.

She sat in front of the computer, her privileges restored, checking e-mails and "legally" gambling. She was day-trading, and the market was working in her favor.

"Jackpot!" She jumped up, yelling and dancing.

"What is it?" her dad asked, running into her room. "What happened?"

"Who's your favorite child?" she asked, pointing to the computer.

"You know girls are daddy's girls, but don't tell your brothers I said that." He made his way over to the desk.

"And don't tell Mom I just made you three big ones. She'll be mad because she doesn't want me 'wasting time' trading."

"Three hundred dollars? How did you do that? The market just dropped yesterday. I could've sworn it was in a rut—"

"Not three hundred dollars. Three *thousand*!" Jacobi informed him, excited.

Her father picked her up and spun her around. "Name it."

"What?"

"Name it. Whatever you want, it's yours." He put her down.

She knew not to move too quickly. "I'm fine, Dad. I don't need anything. Really, I just love the rush of it."

He looked her in the eyes and she felt really guilty for manipulating him. He beamed proudly. "Jacobi, you never cease to amaze me. In fifteen years you've never let me down." He smiled. "And I'm not just saying that because of the money. I love how you go after things. You don't limit yourself, and that's why I don't stop you from trading. You have your camera and the stock market." He shrugged. "Who would've known?"

"I know." She hugged him, not only because she felt bad, but because she knew he meant every word.

"At the rate you're going, you'll have all our stuff paid off. And that's a good thing, because I'm getting another car." He kissed her cheek. "I know you're on punishment, but here," he said, handing her her cell phone. "I've got to run out for a few minutes. Make sure you call me if you need anything. And don't leave . . . the neighborhood."

Time moved slowly as Jacobi waited for Shooby to return her call. She had things to do, and he was holding her up because she couldn't make her next move without him. Executing the next part of the plan was crucial, and she needed to get to the store before her father got home. She knew he'd told her not to leave the neighborhood, but if he believed it was for an urgent reason, one he wouldn't want to deal with, he wouldn't mind; he'd always trusted her to do things she wouldn't normally be able to do when *that lady* was around. It was a part of their truce; she and her father did each other favors they knew *that lady* wouldn't approve of, like when he gave her back her cell phone and she made money for him on the market. She increased his worth and, in turn, he made her happy by giving her more freedom than her mother allowed.

The grocery store was packed. Too many people for the afternoon, Jacobi thought. Teenagers lingered and loitered as if it were Saturday at the mall. The girls she didn't mind so much, but the boys . . . *Dang.* It was like everywhere she went, there they were. She couldn't shake them for the life of her. And she needed to.

"Hey, Jacobi!" a male yelled from behind.

She jetted in the opposite direction, not caring who the voice belonged to. She was embarrassed, and hadn't yet put anything in her cart. She perused the aisles with as much speed as she could muster, pretending to look for things that she hadn't planned to buy. Still, it felt as if everyone were looking, as if they knew what she was shopping for.

A hand tapped her shoulder. "Wait up, Jacobi. Where're ya running off to?"

She turned slowly. It was Malone. Curiosity moved through her. She thought he was supposed to be at the beach with everyone else, and she wondered why he wasn't. But she didn't dare ask. She didn't want to open the door for his questions. By now she was sure Alissa had told him she was on punishment, and why, and she didn't feel like explaining. More importantly, she didn't want him to know why she was at the store. She winced inside. Even though Shooby was the hot topic in her life, Malone's perfection and star power got to her. She wanted to expose only her good side to him; not the sneaky part of her she was now exercising. She smiled despite her dismay. "Oh, nowhere. I just need to pick up a couple of things for the house . . . for my mom." She laughed uneasily. She still wasn't a pro at lying, and she knew they both knew her mom wasn't home. "Things she told me to have when she gets back."

"Cool. I have to pick up some things to get me through the weekend while I'm home *alone*. Mind if I join you?"

Jacobi had no idea what he was up to, but whatever it was, she wasn't having it. She had to get to Shooby. "Look, Malone, if this is some sort of game or setup to get me caught—because you and I both know I'm on punishment—and my mother has you watching me . . ."

He held up his hands in surrender. "No games, I promise. No one has me watching you. And even if they did, I wouldn't tell. I just wanna talk, that's all."

She eyed him for a minute and did a quick comparison. He was Hollywood cute and a professional; Shooby was popular and fine. Malone was a good guy; Shooby was skating on the edge of bad—a definite hook for a girl. But Malone was a bit different today. He wasn't his usual all-eyes-on-me self. He was still dressed in the latest clothes: cut-just-right jeans, hot down-played sneakers, and a loose shirt. He was dressed differently, but that still didn't make him Shooby. But why did Malone make her feel so uncomfortable in her skin? she wondered. Why did she feel like running home to remake herself—both her appearance and her character—to seem like a better person for him?

"So talk." She resumed walking the aisles.

"I was just wondering if you'd like to go somewhere with me."

"Where?" she asked, realizing that she didn't know much about Malone, other than him being on television.

He moved her away from the cart and took over pushing it. "Just somewhere. I mean, why not? We're stuck home while everyone else is having a good time."

She felt stupid. She hadn't even considered that he wanted to go to the beach house; she assumed he was home because he wanted to be. "Not everyone. My dad's home." She shrugged. "I don't know if he'll let me," she said.

"Well, if you change your mind . . . ?" he said, looking at her like he could see through her and her plan.

Jacobi stopped and deadpanned him. "Malone, please." She didn't know who he thought he was, gaming her. She'd heard about his type, and knew he just wanted to use her up. Perfect guys like him didn't fall for girls like her. "Turn here," she directed, ignoring his offer. She looked left and right, wondering if she could send him on a mission somewhere else in the store. She didn't want him to be with her, but he stuck by her side. "Okay," she said as they approached the aisle she'd planned on going down alone. It was obvious that she wasn't going to get rid of him, so whatever he saw, he just saw. She shrugged.

"Please, what? You're dangerous in a good way, Jacobi. You just don't know it. You're intelligent, pretty, you've got a good head on your shoulders, and you're creative."

God, did he sound like her parents. "Thanks, but I'm kinda seeing someone," she said to throw him off. It wasn't entirely true, but her heart did belong to Shooby. Plus, she needed him to back up. She'd been watching him from day one, and he was too tempting. "And I got a lot of work to do. I think there're some film workshops . . ." She stopped mid-aisle, grabbing several packages of feminine pads and dumping them in the cart.

Malone's eyes shifted as he glanced around. A look of disbelief masked his face and his jaw dropped slightly.

"What's the problem, Malone? Is it that I probably

can't go with you, or that I put all of these feminine products in the cart?"

"I'm good." He smiled, picked up a package of pads, and scribbled on it. "That's the address where I'll be this weekend, if I'm not home. Stop by the crib first, and if I'm not there, come by this address," he said, pointing to the maxi pads. "Better yet, just call me to come get you if you change your mind."

Jacobi laughed, still in disbelief that he wrote an address on a package of maxi pads. "Since you were man enough to ask me out, you should be man enough to keep trying. Aren't you going to help me to the counter?" Jacobi asked lightheartedly. She was joking, but, in a way, she thought *why not?*

Jacobi put the second part of her plan in motion when she heard her father enter the house. As soon as the front door closed, she moaned as loud as she could to make sure he could hear her. Balled up in the fetal position, she yelled for God's help when she heard her father talking under his breath. She paused, listening for the direction of his footsteps. He walked toward his bedroom, and Jacobi jumped at the sound of a slamming door followed by a stream of mumbled curses.

"What's gotten into that girl?" He shut another door.

She smiled, knowing that phase two of her plan was in full swing as his steps grew closer to her bedroom.

"Oh God!" she yelled at the top of her voice, rolling around in mock pain.

"Jacobi, you okay?" he asked from the hallway.

"No, Daddy," she lied, slipping the endearment on like a comfortable shoe. She hadn't called him Daddy since before she became an official teenager, and she knew it would warm his heart. There was one other thing she'd planned that she knew would affect him. She was playing a dirty game, and had every intention of going all the way.

"Jacobi, there's a lot of women's *stuff* in the bathroom that wasn't there before," he said as he entered, "and *every*where else. Both the bathrooms are flooded with . . . with . . . stuff. Did your mom come back early?" He stopped short of her bed and stared at the floor.

A trail of white pills led up to the open bottle of Midol. She'd overdone it a bit, and hoped he wouldn't catch on. The path was too staged, as were the open packages of tampons and maxi pads.

"Oh God, Jacobi. Not you, too. You're so young." He wiped his forehead with the back of his hand.

She held her breath to prevent herself from laughing. Clearly, her dad knew nothing about women other than they were, well, women.

"How many did you take?" He held up the pain relievers.

She held her stomach and jerked. "Not enough. No one told me it'd hurt so much. You should've seen all the—"

"Never mind, I've heard enough. I'm calling your mother—she should be here for this, not me."

"But, Dad-deee, she's not taking any calls. I tried already. I think she's lost her phone signal."

"What about Alissa's? You called over there yet?"

"Remember, that's who Mom went with." She still rocked in pretend pain. "I don't know what to do. I don't know how I can bear this pain, and there's still a couple of days of my cycle left."

"Well, I don't see why you should sit around here and babysit me. It's supposed to be your weekend away—you should be with friends and around a woman. You know I'd help you if I could . . ."

"I can call Katydid from the old neighborhood. Her mom won't mind."

He kissed her cheek carefully, as if he were avoiding touching the bed, which was also strewn with women's stuff. "If it's a problem, let me know. I got an important meeting to go to in a half hour. I can take you when I get back, but I don't know when that'll be."

Jacobi rolled side to side. "No, don't worry about it. I'll just catch the bus."

Her father shook his head. "I'm not comfortable with you getting on a bus in your condition. We'll have to find another way, or we'll just have to get through this ourselves," he said, gulping.

Jacobi could tell that he didn't want to deal with the situation, but would because he was a parent. She couldn't let that happen, so she did what she was doing best today—working her way through her problems. "I can ask Malone, Alissa's brother. He's home."

Relief spread across her father's face. "Okay. Tell him I'll give him gas money. The important thing is that you have someone to help you. I don't know what the heck

your mother was thinking, leaving you here like this."
He bent over and kissed her cheek. "Feel better, and call
me when you get to Katydid's. I'll see you in a couple of
days."

"Thanks, Daddy. You've been a big help . . . more than
you know," she said as he closed her bedroom door.

As if her father's exit was a cue, the phone rang.
Shooby's name registered on the caller ID, and her heart
switched from beating to total meltdown. She was completely absorbed in his voice and his every word. She
hung on to thin air just waiting until he spoke again. A
half second was too long.

"So you got the first part of the documentary edited?"
he asked.

"Yeah. I'll bring it over," she said, telling the truth. It
wasn't as tight as she'd like, but it was all she could do
until she was finished filming. "We can look it over when
we get to the beach house. We can ride together. I've got
enough for the bus, or maybe we can pay someone to
give us a ride from the hood. Okay?"

"Cool," Shooby said, his voice coming through the
phone smoothly, making Jacobi smile. "Come through
after eight." Then there was silence. It was if someone
had covered the phone with something, and Jacobi could
hear only muffled sounds.

She tilted her head as if it would help her hear better.
"Huh? Shooby, what did you say?"

Background noise surfaced again from Shooby's end,
telling her the connection was better. "Meet at seven.

You know what it is," he whispered, and then the line went dead.

Jacobi nodded. She got the message. The flash mob was meeting, and he obviously didn't want someone to hear.

# GETTING TO THE GOOD PART

# 20

# KASSIDY

Kassidy moved through her room with speed. She was so excited, she didn't know what to do. She'd finally snagged an opportunity to do a major photo shoot, on location with Diggs. She smiled. She hadn't really gotten the gig. Not yet. But she was sure with a little persuasion—by showing up in clothes like the ones Carsen's mom had given her to wear, but designed by the fashion designer whose set it was—she could pull it off. If not, she'd at least make herself known as a model who wanted to work; that's what Ms. Rosschild had told her after receiving word that right now they were only taking male models. *Right now* being the operative words, Kassidy assured herself. They would eventually hire her, and when they did, she'd be ready. She was making herself available beforehand, and she knew it was touchy. Normally, showing up and trying to get hired went against the rules. But, fortunately for Kassidy, they hadn't given a definite no to female models. She grimaced, wondering if she was taking the right outfits. With two suitcases filled to capacity, she still didn't feel she had packed enough. It was a career hazard, she told herself. No model ever felt like she had a sufficient amount of clothes.

Yummy leaned against the doorway. She tossed a handful of chips into her mouth and chased them with orange soda. She watched Kassidy and loudly rattled the potato chip bag.

"What do you want, Yummy?" Kassidy stopped searching through the room for more things to pack. She put her hands on her hips and impatiently tapped her foot.

"A thank-you would be nice," Yummy said, still chewing.

Kassidy rolled her eyes. What had Yummy done to deserve thanks, besides disappearing into her room from time to time and giving Kassidy's eyes a break from Yummy's disastrous looks and attitude? "For what?"

Yummy stuck her index finger into her mouth, scraping the roof. She clucked her tongue. "Potato chips were stuck," she said, then took another sip of soda and sloshed it around. "You should thank me for not telling on you when you didn't come home. That's what."

Kassidy blinked slowly to avoid giving Yummy an eye roll. She knew the only reason Yummy hadn't told was that she was probably out late herself, hanging out with Romero and doing only God knew what. "Thanks," she said dryly. "Now leave."

Yummy didn't move. "You know I saw Faith yesterday. That's your friend who was supposed to be out of town until today, right?"

Kassidy nodded. She didn't know what was up with Yummy, or why she always wanted to start trouble. They both knew Faith was out of town until today; they'd already had words about it. "Okay, just to entertain you, spill. What happened when you saw Faith?"

"It's not what happened when I saw her that should concern you. It's where . . ." Yummy stood straight and a serious expression spread across her face. "Look, Kass, you don't have to believe me. But I'm telling you, that girl is not your friend. If anything, she wants to be you, and that's not good."

"Whatever. You're just jealous that you don't have any friends." She took an ugly shot at Yummy, knowing her stepsister was running on empty in the friends department.

Yummy grimaced. "Maybe so, but at least I know I don't have many friends. You, on the other hand, don't know an enemy when you see one. And that girl's your enemy . . . you should've seen her yesterday, walking around dressing like you, hair cut like yours . . . everything."

Kassidy's phone rang, and Faith's name and picture appeared on the screen. "Every time you speak of her, she pops up. Early karma, maybe?" Kassidy asked, then accepted Faith's call. "What's good, Faith?"

"Hey! I'm back, and we're in full effect. Ready?" Faith asked from the other end, the wind blowing audibly into the phone.

Kassidy cringed. After hopefully landing the shoot with Diggs, she'd forgotten about meeting up with Faith. She looked at her watch. She could fit in a couple of hours before she had to leave. "Yes, I can't stay out long, though. When do you want to meet up?"

Faith laughed, then blew her horn. "Look out the window."

"Don't trust her, Kass," Yummy warned again, as Kassidy made her way out of the house.

There were two things that Kassidy immediately noticed when she saw Faith. One, Faith's hair was cut in almost the same style as Kassidy's. Two, Faith's car was a mess. An empty coffee mug sat in one of the cup holders, a brush and small makeup bag in the other. Papers and a mustard-colored folder with *Contract* written on it were lying on the passenger-seat floor, and clothes and shoes decorated the backseat. Kassidy drew her brows together, wondering how in the world Yummy knew about the haircut, and how her friend could function in such a mess. She'd read once that a person's surroundings mirrored their life. Could Faith's life really be this messy? Kassidy wondered, still thinking about what Yummy had told her and trying to decide if she should believe her stepsister. She shrugged. She and Yummy had seen Faith on Skype, so maybe Faith had had the cut then, and Kassidy just hadn't noticed it.

Faith's phone rang, and Kassidy looked over at it sitting on her lap. She was shocked. She and Faith were starting to have too much in common for comfort, and it disturbed her. Faith had not only bought a cell just like hers, but she'd also purchased the exact same protective case. Faith looked at the screen, shook her head, then set it facedown on her thigh. The ringtone kept playing, and Faith bopped her head to the song. Kassidy listened to it closely, unsure if she'd heard it before. But there was something about the vocals, one voice in particular, that intrigued her. Then the music stopped.

"My ringtone's hot, huh?" Faith asked, stopping at a red light.

Kassidy nodded. "Yeah. I wanna say it sounds familiar, but I'm not sure."

Faith laughed. "Just like you, Kassidy, to think you've heard something that hasn't been released yet. It hasn't even been leaked on the Internet . . ."

Kassidy quickly spun her head and gave Faith the side eye. What was that supposed to mean, *just like* her? she wondered. "So how was New York? You loved it, right? I mean, I know you've been before—any model worth her salt has. But you stayed a minute, so your shoots had to be fantastic, right?" she asked, changing the subject. If Faith had an issue with her, she wouldn't be taking her to meet industry people, Kassidy told herself.

Faith pressed the accelerator and merged into traffic. "New York was good. In addition to the agent you connected me with, I bagged a lot of numbers and met a lot of people. You know, industry people and *dudes*." She turned and winked. "And I got the hush-hush on a go-see. I hooked up with someone on the inside of the agency who all but promised me a shot. Who knows, around this time next month, I may not just be your biggest competitor, I may move up in the industry and take your spot," Faith said, laughing. "Yes, things are looking up."

Kassidy counted to ten, trying to keep her tongue in check before she spoke. That was Faith's second dig at her, and she felt it deep inside, so there was no mistaking it. She trusted her gut instinct. And what her intuition hadn't forewarned her about, Faith's pokes did. It was one thing to accuse her of knowing a song that hadn't yet been released, but showing her competitiveness was another. Kassidy didn't fight for the spotlight, and she'd never been one not to share it. She looked at Faith and shook her head. Here she'd hooked Faith up with a top New York agent, and Faith had the nerve to be competitive. "Really?" Kassidy asked with a knowing smile.

Faith smashed the brakes, and the car jerked to a stop. They were on the 405 freeway, otherwise known as a parking lot during rush hour. Banging on the horn, Faith's frustration with traffic showed on her face as the wind whipped her hair. The sun's rays warmed Kassidy's skin and she looked up, glad that they were in a convertible. The highway might be jammed, but she didn't care. The view was wonderful, and all the different kinds of music and languages could be heard from nearby cars and their passengers. She took a moment to take it all in. Faith had frustrated her to the point that any other distraction was welcome.

"Yes!" Faith said as the lane next to them opened up. She tugged on the steering wheel, forcing the car into the open space, then eased up on the accelerator as the convertible crawled behind the cars in front of them.

"Geesh!" she complained when the traffic stopped. "This is one thing I hate about Cali. Traffic."

Kassidy just shook her head.

"Faith! Faith? Is that you?" a female's voice called out from the car next to Kassidy.

Kassidy and Faith turned to the right. Kassidy's eyes bulged at the sight of blue hair. The receptionist slash salesgirl sat in a convertible MINI next to them. Kassidy looked left and saw Faith's face had frozen and taken on an ashen appearance.

Blue-haired girl waved. "Didn't think I'd see you again before you leave for New York. Tomorrow, right?" The girl nodded, answering her own question. "Anyway, good thing I did. We got Diggs all taken care of, but you forgot to sign one of the contract pages last week . . ." she explained, then stopped when her eyes connected with Kassidy's. "Oh . . ."

"Oh, what?" Kassidy asked, locking eyes with the receptionist. She wanted to inquire about Diggs, ask Faith how long she'd known him and when they'd started working for the same company, but she didn't. The blue-haired receptionist had given her all she needed. She'd confirmed that, like Yummy had warned, Faith had been in California last week, not in New York like she'd pretended to be.

Blue-haired girl smiled. "Nothing. I just wouldn't have expected you two . . ." She trailed off again.

Kassidy turned to face Faith and saw she was shaking her head *no* at the receptionist. She spun back to the girl, not wanting to miss a thing.

"You're a better sport at this than me. I'll say that," blue-haired receptionist girl said to Kassidy, then her face began to fade from view.

Faith pressed the accelerator as traffic began to move, zipping the car down the freeway. "Guess she must've mixed up when I was going to and coming from New York," she said, her face expressionless.

Kassidy stopped the glare she felt heating her eyes and replaced it with a bright, cheery look. She knew what Faith was doing because Kassidy had done it all the time herself. Faith was playing a part, getting into character and summoning the right expression, just as if she were in front of the lens. But Kassidy had had more practice; she'd been in the modeling profession longer and could fine-tune her acting abilities as if she were on the big screen. That's what had given her a leg up in the industry; not just her looks. Kassidy knew how to transform herself into anything the photographers desired. If they wanted her to cry, she could. If they wanted her to be angry, she'd be vexed. And if they told her to act as if she were the happiest, most clueless person on the earth, she would act like she was acting now. Unaware, with a big cheesy grin on her face.

"Guess so! Congrats on the contract. You didn't tell me about it," she said cheerily.

Faith shrugged. She wore a look of relief. "Oh, that was a while ago," she lied.

"Okay," Kassidy said, then scrolled through her phone, pretending to check her messages. "Sorry, but I have to get home to pack for an on-location. My mom just sent me a text."

Faith's eyes lit. "Really? You didn't tell me about it. Where?"

Kassidy decided Diggs had been right—she did talk too much, and there was no way she was going to tell Faith anything. Yummy had also been correct: Kassidy couldn't trust Faith. Now she just had to figure out how to catch her.

# 21

# *JACOBI*

Jacobi slid clothes hangers back and forth across the closet bar, looking for something to pack. This weekend was going to be the biggest weekend of her life, and she had to look her best. But what was she going to wear? She'd never really cared so much about clothes before, didn't really see what the big deal was. As long as she had her upcoming career—day-trader and/or film maker—she was fine. But whatever she was going to take, she knew she'd better move quickly. She didn't want to risk being home when her dad returned, for fear he'd change his mind.

A loud banging noise coming from the front of the house made her jump. Paranoid, she looked around and almost hit the floor. Then she remembered where she was. There was no violence here. No gunshots ringing out or helicopters hovering with spotlights flashing down on people running from the law. Here, police didn't bust down the wrong door while trying to apprehend a criminal. "Coming. Coming!" Jacobi yelled, wondering if something were wrong with the doorbell. "I said, I'm coming!" she screamed at the top of her lungs, trying to get whoever it was to stop pounding on the door. Jacobi opened the door and locked eyes with Kassidy.

"Where's Diggs?" she asked, her hand on the door, pushing what little weight she had against it.

Jacobi stepped back, opened the door all the way, and allowed Kassidy to enter. She'd never seen her so frantic, except that time in the shoe department, and it worried her. Kassidy had always seemed so cool after that. "Come in. You okay?"

Kassidy walked inside, looking around. She nodded. "Is your brother here? I need to talk to him."

Jacobi pressed her lips together and closed the front door. She began walking to her room and beckoned for Kassidy to follow. Kassidy had promised to help her with her boy problem the day they'd met, and, right now, she needed her to make good on it. "Come on."

Kassidy followed on Jacobi's heels. "Look, Jacobi, I don't mean to be rude, but I really need to see your brother."

Jacobi walked to her closet and began her search for proper clothes again. "He's not here."

"What? Where is he?" Kassidy asked, sounding exasperated.

Jacobi looked at the clock on her dresser. She really didn't have time for Kassidy or Diggs, but, because she was Kassidy's friend, she'd entertain her for a few minutes more. It'd cost Kassidy, though. "Look, Kassidy, I don't know any other way to say this. If you want me to help you, you have to help me. I have to find some clothes for the beach house—"

Kassidy raised her brows and put her hands on her hips, looking extra confused. "Wait . . . I thought you weren't going. That's what Alissa said. I'm sorry you can't go." She wore an apologetic look.

Jacobi was a bit emotionally overcome, and couldn't help but reach out and give Kassidy a quick, sisterly hug. "Aw, thanks for being sorry for me. I appreciate it. Alissa was half right, and she wasn't lying. I wasn't supposed to go—punishment, remember? But I'm sneaking up, and hope my mom and brothers don't—"

"Don't what? Is that where Diggs is?" Kassidy asked, cutting her off and pushing her away. "Look, I know we're cool and all, but I don't want to feel your breast-esses on me," Kassidy said, laughing.

Jacobi looked down at her chest and smiled. She'd been so focused on Shooby, filming the flash mob, and getting to the beach house, she'd forgotten about her begging God for breasts and womanhood. She rocked back and forth on her toes. "Sorry about that. Didn't mean to breast rub. Now about my brother. Maybe he is, maybe he's not. Tell you what: you make good on helping me get Shooby, and tell me why you're so frantic, and I'll give you all the Diggs info you need."

Jacobi sat in the passenger seat of Malone's car with more confidence than she'd ever had in her whole life. Kassidy had hooked her up, and it showed in Jacobi's clothes, look, and attitude. She now had an overnight

bag and backpack full of outfits and shoes, straight hair
that hung past her shoulders, a flawlessly made-up face,
and arched eyebrows. Jacobi's eyes went down to her
breasts. *Yes!* she thought, Kassidy was right; she had
blossomed up top. She was excited and wanted to look at
them all day, but she played it off. She didn't want Malone to know she was admiring her own body. "I don't
know how to thank you for the ride," she said, then
pulled on the door handle to let herself out.

"You gonna be all right?" Malone asked, holding his
finger over the automatic lock button on the driver's side
door.

Jacobi smiled, tsk-tsking him. He was gorgeous—so,
so cute, but she knew he wasn't for her. She just wasn't
his type. "I'm good. I used to live around here, ya
know?"

Malone spread his lips into a half smile. "You're looking extra nice—too cute to be alone. Let me walk you, at
least—"

"No!" Jacobi accidentally yelled, then caught herself.
She didn't want Malone to realize she didn't want him
knowing where she was going, in case her father got to
him. She grabbed her overnight bag, manually unlocked
the door and got out. "I'm good," she said as calmly as
she could. "I only have to cut through those buildings,
and I'm there," she said, pointing, then turned and speed
walked to Shooby's.

Her phone read 6:45 PM as she made her way to the
back door. She raised her hand, knocked softly four times
and waited. Nothing. Again she rapped her knuckles
against the wood, listening for footsteps on the other

side. Still there was no sound. Jacobi looked at her watch, second-guessing the time she knew was correct on her cell. Shooby lived in a duplex, so she had access to three sides of the building. Thinking he was still prepping for the meeting, she decided to peer through his bedroom window. Maybe he was still in there and hadn't heard her knocking. Hiking the strap on her overnight bag higher on her shoulder, she made her way around. Before she reached the side of the place, she could hear commotion. It sounded as if someone were arguing. Jacobi exhaled. She hadn't had to deal with any kind of drama since moving, and she wasn't up for it. She only hoped it wasn't the flash mob. They couldn't make an impact on the world, show America how ridiculous high prices and energy waste were, if they were at odds. More importantly, Shooby wouldn't be able to get his message out to the community. He wanted to show them how much money they were tricking off on designer clothes, sneakers, jewelry, cars and rims, instead of investing in education and business ventures.

"Get outta here with that mess, Katydid!" Shooby's voice blared through the open window, making Jacobi pause in her tracks and listen intently. She had no idea what Shooby and Katydid were arguing about, but she'd never heard so much anger in his voice before, and it worried her.

"No, deadbeat. You get outta here. It's not only *my* responsibility," Katydid shot back. "I didn't do it by myself!"

Jacobi crinkled her brows, wondering what her best friend hadn't done alone. She eased closer to the open window, knowing she shouldn't be eavesdropping, but she couldn't help it. The last thing Shooby had warned her of was to stay away from Katydid. He'd said Katydid was a liar and gold digger, and had been sleeping around. Those hadn't been his exact words, but that's what her ears had heard when he said Katydid didn't know who fathered her baby.

The sound of glass shattering and thumping noises pulled Jacobi out of her curiosity and moved her to the back door. It sounded as if Katydid and Shooby were physically fighting. Standing there listening to them wasn't going to stop them. She couldn't let her best friend and the love of her life tussle, not without intervening. Dropping her overnight bag on the small square concrete slab, Jacobi put her hand on the knob and tried to turn it. She let out a sigh of relief when the door opened. Quickly and quietly, she moved through Shooby's duplex, making her way to his room.

"It's your baby, too," Katydid said, her words stopping Jacobi dead in her tracks as soon as she opened the bedroom door.

She was stuck. She didn't know what to say or feel. Katydid was her best friend—at least Jacobi had believed her to be. And if anyone knew how she felt about Shooby, Katydid did. Still unable to move, Jacobi just stood there, her eyes on both of them and her jaw to the floor.

Shooby saw her first. He just looked at her and shook his head.

Katydid turned, looking at Jacobi through crying eyes while she gripped Shooby's shirt. "Cobi," Katydid said, using the nickname she'd called Jacobi since they were five.

Jacobi still didn't speak. She looked from Katydid to Shooby and back to Katydid. Her eyes welled, and her breathing became labored. For the first time in her life, she felt violent. She wanted to hit somebody—Katydid first—but she wouldn't. Unlike Katydid and Shooby— now teen parents—Jacobi refused to become a product of her environment. Her old stomping grounds, she reminded herself. She didn't have to be like them.

Shooby snatched himself away from Katydid's grasp on his shirt and made his way to Jacobi. "Sorry you had to see this," he said as if it were not a big deal. "That's why I told you to come at eight."

Jacobi just nodded, replaying their conversation in her head. He'd said eight at first, then she'd heard him whisper *seven* through the muffled line. Apparently, he hadn't wanted her to come an hour earlier, so it had to have been Katydid he'd been talking to while he covered the phone.

Katydid just stood there, her eyes now on the floor, a wash of shame and embarrassment on her face. "I'm so sorry. I wanted to tell you when I saw you . . . that's why I said I'm sorry. Remember?" she barely whispered.

Jacobi still had no words. A tear trailed down her cheek, and she tried to wipe it away before it fell.

Shooby reached out to her and tried to put his hands on her shoulders. She jerked away. "Cobi, don't act like that. We have so many bigger things to do than this, like the documentary and going away to the beach. We're still going, right? You're still going to finish the film?"

Jacobi laughed. She couldn't help it. Here she'd believed that he'd liked her, too, especially after the kiss, but he didn't. He was only out for himself, what he could get. He'd been using her, and that was more obvious now than anything. Anything except the pain and betrayal that tore into her soul. She'd lost two friends: a bestest girlfriend, who'd been like a sister, and a fantasy boyfriend she'd liked for years. But the fantasy would never become more than a lesson: All dreams weren't good. Some were nightmares.

Before Jacobi knew it, she'd turned around and run out of the duplex. In one swoop, she grabbed the heavy overnight bag as if it were lighter than a feather and made haste through the buildings. She had no idea how she was going to get out of the old neighborhood or where she was going to go. Home wasn't an option, not after she'd lied to her father and said she'd be staying at Katydid's for the weekend. But she didn't care. She'd figure out her answers as she went along. All she knew was that her mother had been right: the old neighborhood wasn't good for her.

Moving down the dirt path between the buildings, where she'd been so excited before, she collided with a shadow and fell backward. Her heart raced, and an uncomfortable feeling overcame her. History of the neighborhood told her that young girls got hurt here in dark places, and some had even been found dead. She tried to get up, but the shadow reached for her, and she didn't know what to do. She opened her mouth to scream, but her voice got caught in her throat. "Please don't," she managed to say.

"Jacobi? Is that you?" Malone said, still reaching for her.

Relief washed over her. "Yes," she said, taking his hand and getting up.

"You okay?" he asked. "You forgot your book bag. I was coming to try to find you so I could give it to you."

"Oh . . . my book bag," she said. She leaned against his chest, cried like a baby, and told him everything that had just happened while he walked her to the car.

"You're coming home with me. We'll figure this out."

# 22

# KASSIDY

She owed Yummy an apology. She knew she did, and it killed her to admit it, but she had to say she was sorry. She'd been mean to Yummy, maybe more than necessary. Kassidy was a walking emotional rollercoaster when she burst through the front door. She was angry at Faith for being a snake, mad at herself for being so trusting, and desperately desperate to talk to Diggs. She was sure he had answers. If only she could make him spill, which wouldn't be easy. He disliked her for her cheating ways.

"Yummy!" Kassidy yelled, storming through the living room. She didn't see her stepsister anywhere around. "Yummy!" she blared again, this time in the dining room. Still, no Yummy. "Where are you, Yummy?" she asked, making her way to Yummy's bedroom door and banging. But the house was quiet.

"What on earth . . . ?" her mom asked, appearing behind her. "I was just in the office talking, and you and your big mouth almost ruined my phone call. What's the problem with you and Yummy now?" she grilled with an annoyed expression.

Kassidy smiled. "Nothing. There's no problem with me and Yummy. Promise. I just really need to see her. Sister business," she added for effect, and partly because it was true.

Her mother put her hands on her hips and smiled. "Well, say so then. I just saw your sister pull up outside. She was learning how to ride that boy's moped."

Kassidy took off running. She had to get to Yummy. Quickly. "Yummy!" she said, making her way over to a confused-looking Yummy. "Thank God you're here," she exclaimed, wrapping her arms around her stepsister.

"Hi, Kassidy," Romero said.

Yummy pulled away. "Get off me! What the heck . . ."

"Hi, Romero," Kassidy greeted, then waved. Before she knew it, she was waving good-bye to him, lacing her arm through Yummy's, and all but dragging her stepsister into the house. "Yummy will be ready in about an hour, Romero. It's kind of important. Come back then, okay?" she asked, not waiting on an answer. "Don't say nothing, Yummy. Just trust me. Please?"

In Kassidy's bedroom, Yummy sat on the bed with an I-told-you-so-look on her face. She listened intently as Kassidy gave her all the info on Faith and the happenings. "I so owe you an apology, Yummy. You were right. Almost exact same haircut, a shoot for the agency that denied me—which I believe she sabotaged, somehow."

"Somehow? Puhleez. That's what I was trying to tell

you the day she picked you up. I saw her walk out of the building the agency is in. She was there."

Kassidy nodded. "I bet you're right. But to be certain, I gotta get to Diggs to find that out. And now she has the exact same phone as I do, including the protective case. Too many sames, if you know what I'm saying."

Yummy threw some chips in her mouth, nodding. "Told you! And you thought I was the enemy. Huh?" she huffed. "Okay . . . so you called me in here for what? Because you haven't apologized."

Kassidy crossed her eyes at Yummy. "I just did."

"Nope! You said you *owe* me an apology. That's not the same thing as giving one."

Kassidy couldn't help herself. She walked to the side of the bed where Yummy sat and snatched the bag of potato chips from her hands. "Stop all the snacking! All you do is eat, eat, eat. Then you get mad at me for being thin— which isn't my fault, by the way. I watch my figure because I'm a model, but, really, I don't have to. I just can't gain weight. Look at my mom if you don't believe me. I don't think she's ever seen a hundred and ten on the scale."

Yummy stood up and snatched the bag of chips back. "You need to mind your own business. Why do you care if I snack or not? And that's still not an apology. That's criticism."

Now it was Kassidy's turn to take the potato chips. "I apologize, Yummy. I'm really, really sorry. You were right." She dropped to one knee, took Yummy's hand in hers, and gave her a puppy-dog look. She laughed, standing again. "And I have a reason to care about all your snacking. It's unhealthy, for one. It makes you mean to people because you've probably always been teased," Kassidy began, looking Yummy up and down. "Okay, maybe not teased. Only a fool looking to get whooped would do that. But you've been talked about behind your back, we both know that." She hunched her shoulders. "Even I did that when I first saw you. I thought and said terrible things about you. I also bet that's one of the reasons you're a bully and have an issue with skinnier girls. And to top it off, Yummy"—she paused—"you're boyfriendless. That can't feel good, especially when I know you like Romero."

Yummy just nodded. "Maybe. But if you tell anyone, it's me and you. And I'll win. We both know it."

"Well, I was thinking there's another way we can both win, and I'm not talking about fighting." Kassidy crossed her arms, waiting for Yummy to take the bait.

Yummy scratched her head. "In your words, Kass, spill. I'm listening."

Kassidy paced the floor of the department store, waiting on Faith. She'd called her and told her she needed to meet up and shop before leaving for the photo shoot. She'd also hinted that the designer was looking for another model, a hook she knew Faith would bite. She looked to her left and saw Yummy hiding between two racks of clothes, looking out for Faith and texting.

"Get through to Diggs yet?" she whispered to Yummy. She turned her attention toward the walkway she knew Faith would have to take to meet her by the store's dressing room. Jacobi had told her that Diggs hadn't left for the beach-house party yet, so she was sure he was somewhere in the area; at least she hoped he was. She was counting on him.

Yummy shook her head. "I didn't get him on the jack yet. But I just texted him, and he texted back. He's going to call in a minute. The phone's on mute, so we're good in that area."

Kassidy nodded and speeded up her pacing. She needed Diggs on the phone like yesterday. They had to connect with him before Faith arrived, and she was due in a few minutes.

Yummy raised her hand in the air, shaking it side to side. "Got him!" she said a bit too loudly.

Kassidy ran over and ducked down between the clothes racks. She grabbed the phone. "Diggs. Look, I know I'm the last person you want to talk to, but I need you. Really badly. And if you can help me . . . I'll pay you. All the money I get from my next shoot is yours."

There was silence on Diggs's end. Finally, he exhaled in frustration. "I don't want your money, Kassidy. Go 'head."

"Look, I think we both know the same person. Faith."

"Yeah. I did some work with her. So what?"

Kassidy sighed. She felt like she was making progress. "Tell me this: Did you meet her at the agency where the blue-haired wannabe model slash receptionist works? 'Cause if you did—"

"That was your job Faith took?" Diggs laughed. "Dang. I knew something funny was going on, and it didn't sound right. The receptionist told me something about a manager calling in and pulling a switcheroo—

switching one model's appointment time with another's so the other girl—I guess you—would seem like a no-show. She never said who, though, and she seemed a little too tickled by it . . . like she was in on it or something."

Kassidy almost dropped her phone. Diggs had just dropped a major bomb on her, and she couldn't understand it. What had she done to Faith to deserve this? She counted to ten, deciding Yummy had been right. Pure jealousy and competition moved through Faith's veins. "I know this is childish, and I hate to ask you—"

"Just ask," Diggs said. "If she did that to you, then I can only imagine what she's done to me. I have something I'm curious about, too—like her standing me up when we were scheduled for New York weeks ago. She made me miss my flight."

Kassidy nodded. She'd dig deeper into that later, but now she needed to handle first things first. "Can you call her on three-way? I have an app on this phone that can record any audio, even telephone conversations. If you can get her to admit to it, that'd help me a lot. I'm only hitting walls here—can't seem to get any work."

Diggs agreed, and Kassidy handed Yummy back her phone just as Faith was almost running toward the dressing rooms. Kassidy saw Faith stop, hold up a finger as if to say *wait a minute*, then walked back the way she came. All the while Yummy sat on the floor between the clothes racks, nodding. Finally, she put her thumb up in the air. "Got her," she mouthed to Kassidy.

"Part two begins!" Kassidy whispered back, and turned to see Faith returning with a fake smile plastered on her face.

"Sorry. Agent, another shoot. You know?" she said, making her way over to the dressing room.

Kassidy was careful. She took Faith's arm and led her to the other side of the clothing section, noticing that Faith's phone and car keys were in her hand. "Okay, so I know this is so cheesy, but I was thinking I may want to take them by surprise. No one will expect me to dress off the rack. And I need to get their attention."

Faith's eyes lit. She nodded in agreement. "You're right. But you never said which agency or designer."

Kassidy randomly selected pieces of clothing, draping them over her arm as she walked. She held up a god-awful purple piece that she wouldn't wear to garden in. "This is so in now. I found out this morning. Got word from Paris. Can you believe it's here?" she said to Faith.

Faith's eyes blinked in amazement. "Are you sure? I dunno about that one."

Kassidy pursed her lips, then reached out and freed Faith of everything she held—clothes, purse, phone, and car keys. "Grab one and hold it up to you. You gotta see for yourself," she urged, dropping Faith's keys on the floor as quietly as she could.

Faith did as she was told, then shook her head. "I don't think so." She hung the garment back on the rack.

Kassidy shrugged, thrusting Faith's stuff back in her arms, minus the cell phone. She then took back the dress that Faith had hung on the rack. "Well, you lose. It's in. The real version will hit runways this season. So I have to get it. If they see me show up in something that hasn't been released yet—here in the US, anyway—I'll def snag their attention." She draped the garment over her arm and made her way to the dressing room. "Oh, about the agent . . ."

Faith was so close on her heels that Kassidy could feel her body temperature. "Wait. I'm coming. I need to try on some stuff, too," she said, following Kassidy into the foyer of the dressing cubicles. "Now, about the agent? You were saying?"

Kassidy went into an oversized dressing room that she knew was reserved for the handicapped. Normally she wouldn't have done so, but she needed the room today. "Go in the one next to this one so we can hear each other," she said, then began undressing so she could try on clothes she knew she wouldn't buy. "Oh . . . the agent." She stopped talking on purpose, then slid into a grossly designed dress.

"Yes, the agent?" Faith spoke loudly from her dressing room.

"Oh my God. Faith, you have to come see this dress! Slip on whatever you're trying on and come over here to tell me what you think. I'll call the agent . . ."

Faith was still hopping into a pair of pants when she entered Kassidy's dressing room. Kassidy looked at her empty hands and breathed a sigh of relief. She needed her empty-handed. "Okay, you were saying?" she asked, looking at Kassidy's outfit like she'd never before seen such an ugly dress.

"One sec. I need help getting into these other two outfits. If you can lend me a hand . . ." she said, taking her sweet time trying on clothes and rambling about nothing as Faith helped.

A loud thump coming from an adjoining dressing room, followed by a "Whew" caught their attention.

"What's that? My purse is in my dressing room," Faith said.

"Probably nothing," Kassidy said, trying to keep Faith's attention. She pulled a dress off over her head, then began putting the outfit on she'd worn into the store. "Okay, so my agent said the designer's looking for another model. This is a cover shoot—"

Three loud knocks banged against the wall, interrupting Kassidy. That was Yummy's cue.

Kassidy looked at her watch and stomped her foot. "Aw, man. Faith, I forgot I have to be somewhere else ASAP. Meet me at the house in the morning, and I'll get my agent on the phone with you." She grabbed her purse and left, running into Yummy, who held up the mustard-colored envelope labeled *Contracts* that she'd snatched from Faith's car, and Faith's phone, which she'd swapped with Kassidy's. "Let's hope she doesn't have a password on it."

Yummy hunched her shoulders. "If she does, I can break it. You learn a lot of things when you don't have friends. I had to have something to do besides eat when I was home alone all these years."

# 23

# *JACOBI*

Jacobi sat on the sofa, confused. She was hurting, physically and emotionally. Her stomach ached badly, and her heart was hurt. Katydid and Shooby had done a number on her, but she knew she had to let it go. They were from her past, and now their friendship was the same—past tense. In a way, she felt sorry for them. Katydid had ruined her life, become a teen statistic, and was having a baby while she was just a baby herself. She didn't understand it. She'd liked Shooby for years, but had never thought about giving herself to him in that way. She wasn't ready for sex or the problems that came with it. Especially a baby. She changed her mind by the minute about her future career, but she was certain about her goals in life. And success and happiness were what she craved.

Malone plopped down beside her, startling her. In the midst of being caught up in her feelings, she'd almost forgotten that she was at his house. His and Alissa's and Alek's house minus their parents, she reminded herself, and tensed. She'd suspected Malone to be a player, smooth with his game, and capable of pulling any girl. But she wasn't any girl, and she wasn't going to let him take advantage of her. No way.

"You want something to drink? A cold towel to wipe your eyes? A shower?" He rattled off questions, looking into her eyes.

Jacobi stiffened. He was too close. "I'm . . . I'm . . . I'm . . ." she began, then stood up. "I gotta go," she said.

Malone stood, too. "Why?" he questioned innocently.

Jacobi just laughed. Like earlier at Shooby's, she couldn't believe the nerve of people who thought she was a fool. She might make barely average grades, but she wasn't stupid. "Look, Malone. You're cute—gorgeous. You're talented with perfect teeth," she said, pointing to his mouth then showing him her braces, as if reminding him. "You're only a teenager and already you're rich. You're on TV . . ." She shrugged. "What else would you want me for, except the one thing I'm not going to give up?"

It was Malone's turn to laugh. "Serious?" He waved his hand over her body like it was a magic wand. "Look at yourself, Jacobi. Maybe if you really looked, you'd see what I do. You're beautiful—where it counts." He touched his index finger to her temple, then toward her heart, careful not to touch her chest. "Ever since I first saw you, you've been on top of your game. You carry a camera, filming. You dabble with stocks. How many creative girls do you know that also know how to play Wall

Street? And why do you think I keep telling Alek to back up? We usually play the who-can-get-the-girl-first game, but I wasn't having that with you."

Jacobi smiled. She'd never considered herself so talented or beautiful. One look into Malone's eyes told her he was being truthful. He really did see her the way he'd described. She blushed and looked down at the floor. She didn't know what else to do. The scene was playing out like something in the movies, and it scared her. What was he going to do next? Get down on bended knee and propose? she wondered.

"Look at me," Malone said, lifting her face up toward his. "I mean it. I know it's all awkward, us being here alone, but you can stay here if you like. You can sleep in my room, and I'll stay on the sofa. That way you won't have to see your dad—whose car still isn't in the driveway, by the way."

A warm feeling moved through Jacobi while she considered his offer. It was tempting, and she didn't want to let on to her father that she'd lied about getting her period just so she could get out of the house.

"Plus it's late. And what if you go home and he pulls into the driveway while you're at the door? What if he catches you?" Malone asked, all of his questions making huge sense to her.

"Sure? I don't know . . . I've never spent the night at a boy's house before. And if Diggs finds out, he's going to kill me—after he kills you. He's protective," she said.

Malone put his hands in his pockets and laughed. "I feel him. If some dude messes with Alissa—as much as we clash—I'd hurt him. But we don't have to worry

about that. I'm not going to bother you, I promise. And
you won't be spending the night at just some boy's house;
you'll be staying over at Alissa's. Think of it that way."

Jacobi's stomach tied up in knots and an intense heat
moved through her. She nodded, feeling the sudden need
to lie down. "Okay. But I'm staying in Alissa's room and
locking the door."

Malone smiled. "Cool. And in the morning, we can
sneak you back into the car so your dad won't see, and
I'm taking you somewhere."

"Where?" Jacobi asked.

Malone bent forward and planted his lips on her forehead. "On our first date."

Jacobi turned from side to side in Alissa's bed. Her
stomach burned and felt like someone was punching her
from the inside. Wrapping her arms around her middle,
she balled up into a fetal position and tried to breathe her
way through it. She moaned as an intense ache overtook
her lower back. "Ooh," she whimpered. She was in desperate need of pain medicine. Ibuprofen, acetaminophen,
aspirin. She'd welcome anything that would make it go
away, she decided, focusing her eyes in Alissa's dark
room, looking for the route to the bathroom. She didn't
want to stub her toe or trip on anything; she was hurting
bad enough as it was, and she couldn't afford more pain.

With all the strength she could muster, she straightened
herself up, got out of bed, and walked toward the bathroom. Before she could put her hand on the knob, it felt
like someone was stepping on her bladder. All of a sudden she had to pee as if she'd been holding it forever. "Oh

God, what next?" she asked, flipping on the light switch and half running to the toilet. She'd barely made it behind the glass partition and pulled down her pajama pants and panties when she began relieving her bladder practically before her bottom hit the seat. "Whew," she sighed, then seemed to pee away most of her pain. Her shoulders relaxed and she breathed easier. She didn't know how urinating could relieve pain, and she didn't care. As long as most of the pain was gone, she was fine, she decided, wiping herself dry. "Oh. My. God." Her heart raced, and she panicked. She had her first period. *In the house with Malone? Serious?* She shook her head. God had a sense of humor.

Jacobi pulled a gob of tissue off the roll, wrapped it around her hand until it became a wad, and placed it on the crotch of her panties. She pulled up her clothes. Thankfully, she knew where Alissa kept all her feminine products. She walked quickly to the cabinets and opened them. Nothing. She shook her head. She was sure she'd picked the right one. "Maybe not," she said, checking the other one. Still nothing. Now she really panicked. What was she supposed to do? she wondered, opening and closing everything that had a drawer pull on it in Alissa's bathroom and not finding one feminine product.

Her heart raced. She knew by now her father was home, and she couldn't just walk in the door, especially this late. She guessed it had to be at least two in the morning or later, and that killed her next idea. Kassidy was probably sleeping, so texting or calling her was out of the question, and the same thing applied to Alissa. Jacobi breathed deeply. She knew what she had to do. Malone was her only hope. And if he liked her like he said he did, he'd help her.

As he'd promised, he was sleeping on the sofa. The television was on, and his cell phone was by his side. He looked so peaceful, Jacobi didn't want to wake him. But she had to. She just couldn't go all night with a wad of tissue in her panties, especially because she didn't want to take a chance and mess up her clothes—or worse, Alissa's bed.

"Malone," she said, shaking him gently.

He awoke with a start. "You okay?" he asked, half asleep.

Jacobi shook her head in the negative, then tears tracked down her cheeks. She didn't know what was up with all the crying and emotional feelings surging through her body lately, but attributed it to womanhood. It must've been the reason she'd hugged Kassidy, she was sure.

"What's wrong?" he asked, sitting up.

Jacobi gulped. "I don't know how to say it . . . but . . . I tried Alissa's bathroom. You know, I got girl problems?" she said, making her statement sound more like a question.

Malone nodded, not seeming the least bit affected. "Okay. No problem. Check my parents' bathroom. My mom keeps a boatload of stuff there." He smiled. "No need to be embarrassed. I remember when I asked my dad why he didn't mind going to the store to get that stuff for my mom, and he said two things: One, everyone knew it wasn't for him. And two: at least he had a woman, which is more than he could say for a lot of his friends. So, Jacobi, as you see, all dudes aren't so lucky."

Malone laughed. "So if you don't find what you need in my mom's bathroom, I'll run to the store to get what you need. I'm my pops's son . . . and you're going to be my girlfriend, anyway. Might as well start now."

Jacobi laughed. Malone was more than perfect—he was all right with her! He was worthy. Despite her once thinking that he was too good for her, Malone had proved that he *was* good for her. He was boyfriend material. It didn't matter that he was perfectly rich, smart, and popular. What counted was that he put her before himself. That was a lot more than she could say for Shooby. "You know what, Malone? I think you might be right. If you keep this up, you will have a girlfriend."

Malone laughed. "Really? Who?"

"Let's just say that she's super talented with a video camera and likes the stock market."

# 24

## KASSIDY

Kassidy waltzed into the modeling agency with her head held high. The blue-haired girl sat behind the reception desk, chewing on a pencil and talking on the headset. Her eyes widened when she glanced at Kassidy. She held up one finger, signaling that she'd be with her in a minute. Kassidy sat down in the adjoining waiting area, tapping her foot and looking at her watch. She hated to be late, and it annoyed her even more when other people were. As if sensing her irritation, Yummy waltzed in mouthing *sorry* and waving her hand at the blue-haired girl like *don't even bother me.* She sat next to Kassidy and smiled. Kassidy looked at Yummy, and Yummy shrugged, tossing back her newly cut hair and grinning between glossed lips. It was amazing what a makeover could do for someone, Kassidy thought, looking at her new and improved stepsister; she'd had a ball recreating Yummy's look.

"I don't know. Romero brought me," Yummy said, batting her long fake lashes. "Diggs said he'd be here, and I believe he will."

Kassidy nodded. "Okay. I hope so. I really need him here for this."

"Hey!" Diggs said, walking in and speaking loudly to everyone.

The blue-haired girl perked up. She waved and gave Diggs the biggest smile Kassidy had ever seen, and she'd encountered many. It was obvious that the girl had it bad for him, and that gave Kassidy the confidence she needed. "One sec," the girl sang to Diggs.

Kassidy rolled her eyes at the girl's blatancy. *Yuck.* "So, Diggs," Kassidy began, but then the cell phone in her purse started vibrating and singing. The ringtone on Faith's phone that had sounded familiar had come to life, and Kassidy had a lightbulb moment. "I do know that ring. I do!" she said, taking the cell out of her designer bag. "Oh. No." She held up the phone, showing it to Yummy.

"Brent? Is that your Brent?" Yummy asked.

Diggs huffed.

Kassidy froze, staring at the screen.

Yummy snatched the phone from her hand, answering it and pressing the Speaker button so they could all hear. "Brent?" she asked, trying to make her voice sound like Faith's.

"What's up? I got your message yesterday. You know I miss you, too, right?" he asked.

Yummy giggled, still trying to mimic Faith. "Mm-hmm," she said. "I think I'm catching a cold, so if I sound funny . . ."

"Oh no, baby. I'm sorry to hear that. Does that mean you won't be able to come back and finish the shoot? I really wish I could do it with you like last time. I don't know how you worked that out 'cause I heard some dude named Duggs was doing it, but I thank you," he said, messing up Diggs's name.

Diggs shook his head. Brent had confirmed all he needed to hear.

"I'm coming. But first I gotta see Kassidy . . ." Yummy said between fake coughs, still disguising her voice.

Brent grunted through the line. "Why are you going to see that trick? After all she's done to you? C'mon now, Faith. You even said so yourself—she slept with your cousin Carsen and half of Cali in less than two weeks. How can you deal with her, knowing she switched appointments with you so she could steal your contract? I don't know how she tricked me, because I thought she was a good girl. I mean, we never went *there*—" Brent paused, then whispered, "I'm saving all this for you."

Kassidy grabbed the phone. "Save it for her, Brent. Save it and give it to her. You two deserve each other."

"*Kassidy?*" Brent asked. "Is that you? What, you're playing on my phone? After you blocked me from your phone and kept sending me straight to voice mail . . ."

Kassidy crinkled her brows. She hadn't sent Brent to voice mail, only blocked unknown numbers. "Not true, Brent. Maybe you should unblock your number . . ."

"What the . . . ? Oh no. Don't tell me . . . ? Hold on,"

he said. The line got quiet. The clicking of buttons could be heard, and Kassidy guessed he still had a BlackBerry. "Oh, this trick didn't . . . Can you believe Faith set my phone to Private? You know that makes your number come up unknown."

Everybody nodded, but it was too late. She looked at Brent's contact picture on Faith's phone. It was a photo of him and Faith kissing, lip to lip. "Take care, Brent. It was nice while it lasted," she said, more angry and disappointed than defeated. She looked over at Diggs, realizing that she'd been over Brent longer than she'd known. It was the not being able to find him that had piqued her curiosity more than anything. She just couldn't live with thinking he'd ditched her, rather than the other way around. It was a player hazard, she told herself.

"Can I help you?" the blue-haired receptionist asked Diggs.

Diggs pointed to Kassidy.

Kassidy waltzed up to the desk. "You can help us. I have proof that my appointment was sabotaged. And if you don't let me speak to your boss, I'm going to let them know that you may have been privy to it."

The girl looked at Diggs as he made his way over to Kassidy. He laughed and nodded. "Yeah. What she said." He pointed again at Kassidy.

Blue-haired girl lost all the warm color from her face. "C'mon, Diggs. You know I might get in trouble . . ."

Diggs shrugged. "Not as much trouble as you'll be in if I tell them you told me I wasn't needed at my next shoot," he threatened warmly. He reached out and put his hand on hers. "Don't make me do you like that. Just take us to the back, and I'll tell them you had nothing to do with it, that we found out another way." He held up the mustard-colored *Contracts* envelope. "Like this . . . We could've just found this."

Kassidy looked at the oversized garage and scrunched her nose. Motorcycles were all around, and she wasn't sure if she'd picked the right place to confront Carsen. She took a glance over her shoulder and saw that all of her supporters were in place. Diggs had come, even though he was supposed to be at the beach-house party already. Yummy stood next to Romero, who had admitted being interested in Yummy after Kassidy told him she'd never view him as more than a pretend brother-in-law. He looked at Kassidy and smiled, his arm around Yummy's shoulder. Yummy was looking like the plus-size model Kassidy was sure she could become with a little more work. Kassidy had three friends to back her up, one of whom was her stepsister—the stepsister she never thought she'd like, and it felt good. It would feel even better when they went to confront Faith next, and Kassidy could switch phones with her. Yes, it felt great. Almost better than clearing up all the confusion that had become her life. She no longer had to worry about an MIA boyfriend, who'd pretty much turned his back on her as soon as her plane left the tarmac and had taken a stranger's word that she was promiscuous. She no longer blamed Yummy for messing up her modeling appointment and snitching to Diggs about all the boyfriends she had. And Diggs no longer believed that she was a loose girl who gave her body to any boy who looked her way.

In fact, he knew she was pure. No, none of those things concerned her anymore. Not even her job situation. Thanks to her own initiative in confronting the agent, she'd landed a go-see, and because of Diggs, she was almost certain that she'd get the Ralph ad.

Her hand banged against the huge garage door. It slid open, and some guy wearing a black motorcycle vest appeared. "Yeah?"

Kassidy gave him a smile that always disarmed guys. "I'm looking for Carsen."

The guy whistled. "Wish it were me. Hold up."

Kassidy looked around. She was still nervous, and hadn't really thought about what she was going to say.

Carsen appeared, smiling and looking as cute as ever. "Hey, Kassidy. What up? Didn't think I'd ever see you here." He walked up to her, reaching out for a hug.

Kassidy stepped back. "Well, you texted me this address when we were going out before. But, listen, I need to ask you something. You know Faith?"

Carsen nodded. "Yeah. Unfortunately."

Kassidy raised her brows and looked back at Diggs. He walked over immediately.

"Oh, so you're with him now?" Carsen asked, cockiness in his voice.

"We're just cool. He came with me to make sure I got here safely," she lied. Diggs had come to make sure she was okay in case Carsen got out of order, but she wouldn't dare say that. That would start a fight. "What do you mean by 'unfortunately'? I thought she was your cousin."

Carsen nodded. "S'up?" he said to Diggs, then turned back to Kassidy. "Who's my cousin? That stalker? Please, man. Faith's no relative of mine." He looked around, then up and down the street. "Matter of fact, if you see her, don't tell her where I am. Don't give her my number. Don't tell her nothing. My moms almost had to call the police to get rid of that girl."

Kassidy's jaw dropped. Faith's mess was getting thicker and thicker by the second. "Speaking of your mom, how is she? She was really nice to me after you dropped me off—left me for dead. I'm sorry, that's a New York expression. I mean when you left me on the doorstep with food poisoning and disappeared, never to be heard from again. It's a good thing we never hooked up," she said, laughing; but she was serious. She needed Diggs to hear for himself that nothing had ever transpired between her and Carsen.

Carsen shrugged. "Well, ya know. We laid the rules down in the beginning. I'm no boyfriend material. I play around too much for that." He looked her in the eye. "Thought you knew that. I was just *in* it to get in *it*." He nodded, then looked at Diggs. "You a dude, ya feel me."

Diggs shook his head. "Nah. Don't know nothing about that."

Kassidy laughed. "You really thought that's what I wanted? Wow. I can't believe that. I never said it." She looked at Diggs. Carsen wasn't boyfriend material, but Diggs was. Diggs didn't play and he didn't share. He was real about his, and Kassidy admired him for it. Diggs winked and she returned it. "What about you, Diggs?" she asked. "What kind of material are you?"

Diggs smiled as cool as he could. "I'm definitely not boyfriend material, either. My moms isn't raising a boy;

she's raising a man. I'm a man about mine. I told you that. So if you're looking for a boyfriend, you gotta look somewhere else. When you want a man, come see me." He pounded his fist on his chest.

"Haaa!" Carsen said. "I like that, partna. I like it in ya!"

Kassidy's eyes bulged and she stared at Diggs. "I'm seeing you now."

# CALI BOYS

## Kelli London

## ABOUT THIS GUIDE

The following questions are intended to
enhance your group's reading of
CALI BOYS.

# Discussion Questions

1. Jacobi's hormones caused physical changes that got in the way of her recognizing her true identity. She didn't see herself as beautiful, talented, or smart. Yet boys found her attractive, she was a filmmaker on the rise, and she traded stocks. Do you think a girl's physical changes during adolescence can affect her self-identity and self-worth? Why or why not?

2. Jacobi, like a lot of girls, was attracted to the "bad" guy. Why do you believe some girls like bad boys instead of guys that are good for them?

3. Jacobi and Kassidy both stayed all night at a boy's house. Were they wrong to do so? Discuss the potential dangers.

4. Jacobi and Kassidy both lied to their parents all in the name of love. Why is this wrong?

5. Kassidy was a self-proclaimed "player" who refused to be true to one guy. Do you think her being a player had a positive or negative effect on her reputation? Does a girl's disloyalty to boys reflect her ability to be loyal to others?

6. Rate your loyalty: Kassidy refused to be tied down to one guy and betrayed every boy she'd claimed

as her own: Romero, whom she didn't really like as a boyfriend, but misled him to think so; Carsen; and Brent. Yet she felt betrayed by Faith for her wrongdoing. Is there a difference between Kassidy's disloyalty and Faith's? Why or why not?

7. Some say once a cheat, always a cheat. Do you think that Kassidy would've cheated on Diggs?

8. *Different* can be a good thing. However, Kassidy and Yummy had their differences and obvious prejudices, and each was judgmental about the other's weight. How do you handle others' differences? Are you open and accepting or judgmental?

9. Do you think Yummy's meanness and bullying ways were a reflection of how she felt about herself?

10. Jacobi's best friend, Katydid, pulled the ultimate no-no. She took Shooby, the boy that Jacobi wanted, and became a teen-pregnancy statistic. Other than abstinence—the guaranteed way to prevent pregnancy—are there other measures a girl can take to prevent such an awful thing happening? Please discuss.

If you enjoyed *Cali Boys*, don't miss

## *CREEPING WITH THE ENEMY*
by Kimberly Reid

Using skills learned from her mom, an undercover cop, Chanti Evans has already exposed lies and made enemies at her posh new school, so she's no stranger to the games people play. But she's learning the hard way that at Langdon Prep, friends can play more dangerous games than any enemy.

Turn the page for a preview of Chanti's adventure . . .

The line in the bodega is five deep because it's Freebie Friday and the tamales are buy-one-get-one. I don't mind the wait—the scent of green chili reminds me how lucky I am to live on Aurora Avenue, just two blocks from the best tamales on the planet, or at least in a thirty-mile radius. Seeing how it's smack in the middle of Metro's second worst police zone, there isn't a lot to appreciate about The Ave, so that's saying something about these tamales. Since they only let you get one order, I always find someone to go along who doesn't love them like I do so I can get one extra. Today my tamale pimp is Bethanie—we're numbers six and seven in line—and she's calling me some choice words for making her wait for a free tamale when she can afford to buy the whole bodega. I'm trying to explain to her that there's no sport in being rich (not that I would know), when a guy walks in from a Ralph Lauren ad and becomes number eight in line.

I don't know how a person could look so out of place and seem completely at ease at the same time, but this guy is pulling it off. He's also checking out Bethanie so hard that even though he's a complete stranger, he makes me feel like I'm the one who crashed the party.

"What's so good in here that people are willing to wait for it?" he asks Bethanie. He pretty much ignores me, so I almost laugh when his line goes right over her head.

"Supposedly the tamales are," she says, "but I wouldn't know."

I'm no pro at the flirty thing, but I'm sure he wasn't expecting her answer to be *tamales*. I move forward in the line, ignore their small talk, and study the five-item menu as though I don't know what to order. Now there are only two people in front of me. Some Tejano music and the smell of cooking food drifts into the store from somewhere behind the clerk. I imagine somebody's grandmother back there wrapping corn husks around masa harina and pork. Yum.

I check out Preppie Dude like I'm not really looking at him but concentrating on the canned peaches on the shelf behind him. Cute. Not so cute he couldn't at least say hello to me before he starts feigning for my friend. He's still the last person in line even though tamale happy-hour runs from four to five and the line is usually out the door until five. Weird, because it's only four thirty. I'm about to mention how weird that is to Bethanie, but she's finally figured out Preppie is flirting with her and has apparently forgotten me, too.

Now there's just one person ahead—Ada Crawford, who lives across the street from me and who I'm pretty sure is a hooker even though I don't have any proof. If we lived in a different neighborhood, I might say she is a call girl since her clients come to her. But we live in Denver Heights, so she doesn't get a fancy title. Luckily she hasn't noticed me behind her because I'm not supposed to be here and I wouldn't want her to tell my mother she saw me. Not that Ada ever has much to say to my mom.

Still no one else has come in. Along with the clerk I don't recognize, maybe they've also changed the cutoff time to four thirty. I suppose the owners would go broke if all people did was come in for the freebie and not buy anything else. Or worse, get a friend to pimp an extra freebie. I place my order—feeling slightly guilty—when I hear the bells over the door jangling, announcing a new arrival, just as Ada walks away with her order. I look back to see a man holding the door open for Ada. He stays by the door once she's gone and just stands there looking at the three of us still in line. He's jumpy. Nervous. He looks around the bodega but doesn't join the line and doesn't walk down the aisles of overpriced food. His left hand is in the pocket of his jacket, and my gut tells me to get out of the store. Just as I grab Beth's arm, the man brings his hand out of his jacket. It's too late.

"All right, everybody stay cool. Don't start none, won't be none. Just give me what's in the drawer," he says to the clerk, pointing the gun at him.

I'm hoping the clerk won't try to jump back and pull out whatever he has under the counter. Every owner of a little mom-and-pop in my neighborhood has something under the counter. Or maybe it's in the back with the tamale-making grandmother. But no one comes from the back and the clerk isn't the owner. From what I can tell, it's his first day and he doesn't care about the money or the shop, and opens the cash drawer immediately. Bethanie pretends she's from money, but I know she's a lot more like me than she lets on. She knows what to do in a situation like this: stay quiet and let it play out. We steal a quick glance at one another and I know I'm right. Either she's been through it before, or always expected it to happen one day.

I'm trying to stay calm by thinking ahead to when it will be over. Ninety seconds from now, this will just be a story for us to tell. The perp will be in his car taking the exit onto I-70. Hopefully I will not have puked all over myself by then. Or worse.

But then the cute guy speaks.

"Look man, just calm down."

What the hell? Just *shut up*, I want to scream. The clerk has already put the money into a paper bag and he's handing it over right now. This will all be over in thirty seconds if Preppie will just shut up.

The perp turns the gun in our direction. I lock eyes with him even though I know it's not the smartest thing to do. He realizes I can identify him; I can see him thinking about it, wondering what to do next. Suddenly, the smell of tamales sucker punches me and my stomach lurches. The wannabe hero turns his back to the perp and shields Bethanie, pushing her to the ground and sending the contents of her bag all over the bodega floor. That move is like a cue for the perp—he breaks our gaze, grabs the paper bag from the clerk, and takes off.

I was right—it's over in just about ninety seconds. None of us wants to stick around to give the cops a statement. Preppie, who might have gotten us all killed, helps Bethanie grab the stuff that fell out of her bag while I scan the store for cameras. There aren't any that I can tell. As the three of us leave the store, the clerk is picking up the phone to call either the owner or the police, depending on how good the owner is about obeying employment laws and paying his taxes. I manage not to puke until I reach the parking lot.